# MILLS

## Centenary Collection

**Celebrating 100 years of romance with
the very best of Mills & Boon**

*First published in Great Britain 2008
by Harlequin Mills & Boon Limited,
Eton House, 18-24 Paradise Road, Richmond, Surrey TW9 1SR*

© Liz Fielding 2001

ISBN: 978 0 263 86709 1

76-0309

*Harlequin Mills & Boon policy is to use papers that are natural, renewable and recyclable products and made from wood grown in sustainable forests. The logging and manufacturing processes conform to the legal environmental regulations of the country of origin.*

*Printed and bound in Spain
by Litografía Rosés S.A., Barcelona*

# A Perfect Proposal

by
Liz Fielding

MILLS & BOON
*Pure reading pleasure*

**Liz Fielding** started writing at the age of twelve, when she won a writing competition at school. After that early success there was quite a gap – during which she was busy working in Africa and the Middle East, getting married and having children – before her first book was published in 1992. Now readers worldwide fall in love with her irresistible heroes, adore her independent-minded heroines. Visit Liz's website for news and extracts of upcoming books at www.lizfielding.com

Look out for Liz Fielding's classic novels *The Ordinary Princess* and *City Girl in Training* in Mills & Boon By Request® available in May 2008 and July 2008, as well as her brand-new book, *The Bride's Baby*, from Mills & Boon® Romance in April 2008!

# CHAPTER ONE

'MARK, what's happened? You were supposed to be at a meeting with the surveyors first thing. They just called from the site—'

'Jane...' Mark Hilliard sounded as if he'd come out of some dark place and needed a moment to gather himself. 'I'm sorry, I should have called... Ring them back and apologise for me, will you? I've got a bit of a crisis at home.'

'Crisis?' Jane Carmichael's heart turned over. 'Is Shuli sick?'

'No, she's fine. But she's just sacked another nanny.'

'*Shuli* sacked the nanny? I know she's bright, but isn't that rather advanced behaviour for a three-year-old? What did she do? Call her into the nursery, sit her down on Mr Fluffy and say, "I'm afraid you haven't lived up to the promise of your excellent references, Mrs Collins. I'm going to have to let you go?"'

'Mrs Collins was the nanny before last.'

'Oh, Mark!' Jane's amusement evaporated rapidly. She'd interviewed Sarah Collins herself and had been convinced she would be perfect for the job.

'She left last month. Some excuse about family problems. You tried so hard that I couldn't bring myself to tell you. The agency has been sending me temps in the meantime. It's given Shuli plenty of opportunity to practise the art of getting rid of them. This morning she just screamed the place down until the poor woman left the house. I don't know why; her references *were* excellent. She seemed perfect in every way to me.'

'Things look different from knee height. It wasn't you

she was giving a bath and tucking up in bed.' Then, grateful that he couldn't see her quick flush, 'Maybe you should try asking Shuli what she wants before you take on someone else. She might settle better with a live-in nanny.'

'She might. I wouldn't.'

They'd discussed it at length before, but he was clearly uncomfortable about sharing his house with a strange woman. She wasn't wild about the idea, either, but Shuli was more important than her own pathetic little jealousies. Getting him to acknowledge that his little girl was an individual who might have feelings of her own was an uphill battle, but someone had to try.

'Has she calmed down now?'

'Like any woman, Jane, she's perfectly happy now that she's got her own way.' Then, somewhat belatedly. 'I'm sorry, I didn't mean you…'

'No.' He didn't think of her as a woman at all.

'The agency is trying to find a replacement and in the meantime I'm calling everyone I can think of to have her.'

'No luck?'

'My mother is away at some conference and my sister moved to Strasbourg last month. They're not your average grandmother/aunt combination,' he said wearily. 'It looks as if I'm going to have to work from home until I can sort something out. At least for the rest of the week. Will you bring over the files on my desk, please? And the mail.'

'Are you sure? It'll be nearly lunchtime by the time I arrive. Maybe you should just take the day off and spend it with Shuli.' That was what the child wanted. A father who was there to give her a cuddle when she needed it. Who had time for her when she woke up eager to play; who made an effort to get home in time to read her a bedtime story. She didn't blame Shuli for sacking a series of strangers, no matter how well qualified, who were being paid to stand in for a mother she'd never known, for a father who found her presence a painful daily reminder of everything he'd lost. 'It's a lovely day,' she pointed out, trying again. 'You could take her to the country park.'

'Not today, Jane,' he said, briskly. 'If I don't get the Arts Centre designs finalised this week we'll fall behind programme.'

Heaven forbid that should happen. 'Of course. I'll be there as soon as I can.'

She called the surveyors to reschedule the meeting, then sat for a moment while she gathered her own protective shell about her. Shuli wasn't the only one who longed for Mark Hilliard to notice her. Love her.

But she was a grown-up, twenty-four years old, and, since she was also in her right mind, flinging herself onto the floor and screaming for attention wasn't an option.

She was good old Jane, who could always be relied on no matter what the crisis. The perfect secretary, hiding her love for her heartbreakingly handsome boss behind her owl-like spectacles. A total cliché.

Okay, forget the spectacles. But she might as well wear them for all the notice he took of her.

But Mark Hilliard was irresistible. Ever since she'd sat across his desk for the first time and seen him, newly bereaved, grief in every dark shadow of his ravaged face, with his baby daughter in a carry seat beside him, she'd known it would be a mistake to stay.

There had been an urgent phone call moments after she'd arrived for the interview. She'd picked up the noisy infant, taken her into Reception and played finger games with her while her father had dealt at length with some crisis.

When he'd finished, he'd come looking for her. 'You've got the job.'

The heart-leap of joy had been a warning and she'd heeded it. Much as she'd wanted the job, she knew that falling in love with the boss at first sight, any sight, was always going to end in tears. Hers.

'But you know nothing about me,' she'd said.

'I know that you see what needs to be done and do it. That's good enough for me. Can you start now?'

Shuli had been sitting on her lap, playing with the buttons on a smart new suit bought specially for the occasion. Well, it had looked smart in the shop. On her it didn't have quite the same stylish appearance. Nothing ever did; she just wasn't a standard size. Not tall enough. Not anything enough. And now it had dribble marks on the lapel.

'Not promising material. Lacks that touch of class.' That was what the woman at the secretarial agency had written on her application form. Jane was very good at reading upside down. Her skills were excellent but they hadn't even taken her on as one of their temps.

While she had been putting on her coat a call had come into Reception. Mark Hilliard, of Hilliard, Young and Lynch Architects, needed a first-class secretary urgently.

As soon as she'd reached the pavement she'd called him on her mobile phone. She sounded better than she looked and he'd asked her to come over right away.

He hadn't been put off by her appearance. She might have loved him just for that. Which was why, even though every sensible bone in her body had urged her to take a job that she wanted, needed, some internal alarm system had rung loud bells, warning her to turn him down, walk away.

There would be other jobs. Safer jobs. Jobs where her heart wouldn't be on the line every minute of every working day. But Mark had looked so desperate. And Shuli had smiled so winningly at her.

Which was why, for more than two and a half years, she'd seen what was needed and she'd done it, without waiting to be asked.

All except for Shuli, she thought.

She'd tried to engage his attention in his adorable daughter, but it was clear that he found it difficult to be near her, and for all those two and half years she'd watched helplessly as he'd done everything for the child but give himself. It just wasn't good enough. If he couldn't be a father to the child, he'd have to give her a mother. And, as always, having recognised the need, she would have to organise the solution.

She gathered the files Mark had asked for and picked up her laptop, stopping in Reception to have calls redirected.

Her reflection in a framed picture of Hilliard's most recent project warned her that her hair was escaping from the neat chignon the hairdresser had assured her would stay in place in a force ten gale.

She still needed to work on her presentation. Fortunately Mark wouldn't notice even if she shortened her skirts to her knickers and piled on the make-up. He just didn't see her that way. It was the one thing she had going for her.


'Read me a story, Daddy.'

Mark glanced irritably at his daughter, who was perfectly happy now that the nanny had gone and she'd disrupted his day.

'I'm busy, Shuli.'

She pushed the book she was holding onto the desk. It was old. Much read. 'This story,' she persisted.

Recognising the futility of resistance, he picked up the book. 'Where did this come from?'

'Jane gave it to me,' she said. 'I love Jane. I really, really love Jane.'

'Yes, yes, of course you do...' He opened the first page and saw, written in a round, childish hand, the words 'This book belongs to Jane Carmichael'. It was one of her own precious childhood books, brought into the office to amuse Shuli on those days when he had no choice but to take her in with him. It occurred to him that maybe that was what the child had wanted all along: to see Jane. He glanced at the clock, wondering what on earth was taking her so long.

Shuli crawled up onto his lap. 'Read it now, Daddy.'

'Please,' he said, automatically correcting her.

'Please, Daddy,' she said. And smiled. She was the very image of her mother. He could almost hear her voice pleading with him. *"Please, Mark…let me go…"*

The sound of a car pulling up in front of the house released him from the painful memory as, story forgotten, the child slid down and hurtled towards the door. He followed, opening it, and Shuli flung herself at Jane's knees, hugging them.

'You wouldn't consider swapping jobs would you? You'd be the best-paid nanny in the county.'

'No, thanks. Besides, she doesn't need a nanny.' Jane put down the files and her laptop and picked up the child to give her a proper hug. She got a big sticky kiss back. 'She needs a mother.' She put the child into his arms and took off her jacket. 'I'm sorry I was so long. The traffic was a nightmare. I need coffee. Urgently.'

'Help yourself. You know where everything is.'

She hooked the jacket over the newel post at the foot of the stairs and headed for the kitchen. Putting Shuli down, he followed her. 'What about you?' she asked, turning to him as she filled the kettle. 'Coffee? Or would you prefer tea?'

'Coffee, thanks.'

Shuli was at her knees again, and she looked down. 'What about you, sweetheart? Do you want something to drink?'

She giggled. 'Coffee, thanks,' she said, imitating her father.

'And would that be orange juice coffee, or apple juice coffee?' Shuli giggled as Jane opened her bag and produced a wrapped chocolate biscuit finger. 'And how about this?'

'Is she supposed to have stuff like that?' Mark asked.

Jane glanced up, surprised. 'You don't ever buy her chocolate?'

Her rebuke, mild though it was, took him by surprise.

'Of course not. It's bad for her teeth.' He and Caroline had read all the books. Theirs was going to be the perfectly raised child. No junk food. No eating between meals. No sweets… 'Isn't it?' he asked, suddenly less certain.

'I imagine she has a toothbrush?'

'Yes, yes, of course. I'll, um, be in the study.'

'We'll be right with you.'


Jane placed the tray on the desk out of Shuli's reach and then settled her at a table with a pile of paper and crayons. 'Daddy and I are going to be busy for a while. What I'd like you to do for me is draw a picture that I can pin up in my office. Will you do that?'

'Okay.'

'Good girl.' She turned and saw that Mark was watching her with a faintly baffled expression. She poured the coffee and they went quickly through the morning post. 'I've dealt with most of it.'

'As always. That's it?'

She took a moment to compose herself. She knew what she had to say. She'd nearly missed her exit on the motorway rehearsing her lines.

'Not quite.' He waited. 'There's this.' Heart hammering, she handed him a broadsheet newspaper folded back at an inside page.

*Connections?*' he queried, looking up. 'What is this?'

He couldn't be that dense. Or then again… 'It's a dating column. I've prepared a draft advertisement for you.'

He took the sheet of paper she offered.

'"Widower, 34, with small daughter, WLTM warm, caring woman, N/S, GSOH, for LTR."' He looked up. 'WLTM?'

'Would like to meet.' Seeing his blank expression, she added, 'Non-smoker with good sense of humour for long-term relationship.'

'Oh.'

'On the day you hired me, Mark, you said I was someone who saw what needed to be done and got on with it. That's what I'm doing now. For Shuli's sake. I've written the ad for you. I'll even filter the replies if you want me to. All you have to do is tell me to go ahead and place it.'

He glanced at the newspaper again, read some of the ads. 'This one wants a ''lady of class and intelligence for romance and precious moments''.' He cocked a wry eyebrow in her direction. 'Does that mean what I think it means?'

'Undoubtedly,' she said, absolutely refusing to blush, or to laugh, which was what he hoped she'd do. Laugh and forget it, so that they could move on to the important business of life. Work. She cocked an eyebrow back at him. 'You can draft your own specifications if you'd prefer. Just don't forget the LTR.'

'Jane, please… You can't be serious.'

'No? Your daughter has rejected four perfectly competent, kind and caring nannies in as many months. She's trying to tell you, in the only way she can, that she needs more.'

'More?'

'More than you're giving her. Someone who puts her first. Someone who she knows is going to be there for her every morning when she wakes up, every night to read her a story.'

'I do what I can, but I have to work…' He wasn't laughing now. He couldn't even quite meet her gaze. 'People depend on me. My partners, everyone in the office—you, even. If I don't work, Jane, no one gets paid.'

It was more than that; they both knew it. But if he couldn't, or wouldn't, do the job himself, he must offer a surrogate. 'Then, I repeat, she needs a mother. You are the only person who can provide her with one. I appreciate that finding time to look for yourself is difficult, hence the ad. Or you could use an agency. Lots of people in your situation take this route.'

'Maybe they do. Maybe you're right.' He tossed the advertisement she'd drafted on the desk and then raised one hand in a gesture of helplessness at the silver frame containing a photograph of Shuli's mother. 'I appreciate your concern and I'll give it some thought, but can we move on, please?' He picked up a file.

'It's three years, Mark,' she said, refusing to let the subject drop. 'Caroline would expect you to move on. She'd want Shuli to have what all children need.'

He was beginning to look haunted. 'Where in the world would I find the kind of woman who'd take on someone else's child?'

'It's not that uncommon these days. With the high divorce rate.'

But that wasn't the problem and they both knew it. The problem was that no one could ever be as wonderful as Caroline...as perfect as Caroline...as beautiful as Caroline.

'Very well,' he conceded, finally accepting that she wasn't going to let the subject drop. 'The kind of woman who'd be prepared to accept the one-way relationship which is all I could offer?' That he'd said it out loud, admitted it, was the first step, Jane knew. He glanced at the child, quietly working at her drawing. 'I know you mean well, but I couldn't ask it of any woman. Certainly not one with all the great qualities I'd want for Shuli.'

Jane felt his pain, physically hurting for the man. She wanted to reach across the desk, take his dear face in her hands and tell him that everything would be fine if only he'd trust her...

Keeping her voice brisk and businesslike, she said, 'Don't underrate yourself, Mark. You can offer a lovely home, a comfortable life, friendship. A lot of women would be happy to settle for that.'

'Would they? And how would I know they weren't just doing it for the money? That a year on this "warm, caring non-smoker with a good sense of humour'' wouldn't be suing for a divorce and a big fat chunk of my assets?'

He'd spotted the flaw in her suggestion. She'd been sure he would. Well, he'd look for any excuse to evade the issue.

'I think Shuli could be relied upon to see off any pretenders.'

That, at least, raised a smile. 'Yes, I suppose she would.' He sat back, regarded her across the broad desk. 'You've thought this through, haven't you?'

'Of course. I wouldn't come to you with some half-baked plan.'

'No.' He continued to regard her thoughtfully. 'Tell me, Jane, would *you* settle for a platonic marriage?'

This was it. The opening she'd been waiting for. She swallowed. 'Are you asking me?' she replied, her voice perfectly calm even while her heart was pounding loud enough to be heard in the next county.

'Yes,' he said. 'I want to know if you'd marry a man who wasn't in love with you?'

She shook her head. More hair slithered from the grip of pins unequal to the task. 'No, Mark. That wasn't my question.' He frowned, and she very nearly lost her nerve. It wasn't too late to bottle out... 'My question was...are you asking me if I'd marry you?'

# CHAPTER TWO

THERE was a moment of perfect stillness while Mark Hilliard tried to decide if Jane was serious.

She was sitting opposite him, the way she did every working day of his life. She looked the same. Alert, a smile hovering behind her eyes and waiting to break out at the slightest provocation, totally in control of everything but her hair. And waiting for an answer to her question.

Was he asking her if she'd marry him?

The answer, of course, was yes. In a purely rhetorical sense. But Jane hadn't been speaking rhetorically. She was never anything but totally straightforward. She didn't play games, or tease, or do any of those tiresome female things to get what she wanted. He scarcely thought of her as a woman at all. Which was why she was so easy to work with. To be with.

She'd asked him a serious question and expected him to give her a serious answer. If he said no, she wouldn't be offended. This wasn't about feelings or emotions; it was about a practical solution to a problem that was beginning to affect not just his life but the success of his architectural practice.

And the longer he delayed before dismissing the idea out of hand the less inclined he felt to do so. It did, after all, make the most perfect sense.

He knew her so well. There'd be none of that awkwardness inevitable in any new relationship. None of the risk. She was hard-working, kind, loyal and beneath that serious exterior he knew she possessed in full measure that essential GSOH. She knew him, understood him perfectly, wouldn't expect a thing from him except loyalty and friend-ship.

She'd be the perfect wife for him in every way. Whether he'd be the husband she was looking for was something else entirely.

'Would you consider moving in here?' he countered.

'Give up my job and look after Shuli for you full-time? As what? I'm sorry, Mark. I can see what you'd get out of such an arrangement, but, much as I love Shuli, I don't see it as a great career move for me.' She didn't wait for him to spell out the financial package he would be offering her as his 'home' rather than his 'office' secretary. 'Maybe we'd better stick with the advertisement.'

Shuli, hearing her name, looked up. 'I've nearly finished, Jane.' And she held up her picture for them to see. Three stick figures beside a house. 'Daddy, Jane and me,' she said.

'It's lovely, poppet,' Jane said, amazed that the tremor shaking her from the inside out wasn't evident in her voice. 'Are you going to draw some flowers in the garden?' she asked.

Shuli at least knew what she wanted, and Mark had made an opening offer, although what exactly he was offering he clearly hadn't thought through.

Now she'd give him time to meet some of the women who'd undoubtedly answer his advertisement by the truck-load. She knew that no matter how nice they were he'd recoil from getting sucked into a relationship he couldn't control, with a woman who'd expect more from him than he felt able to deliver.

When she returned to her seat Mark was flicking through his diary, taking advantage of the interruption to change the subject. It didn't matter, she told herself. She'd put the idea in his mind. There would be another day, another upset. She knew how to be patient.

'I've rescheduled the site meeting with the surveyors for

tomorrow,' she said, moving briskly on. 'Nine-thirty. Bring Shuli into the office and I'll take care of her.'

He made a note and then looked up. 'Would next Tuesday suit you?' he asked.

'Next Tuesday?'

'I shouldn't think the registrar will be busy mid-week.' Then, when she didn't answer. 'You don't want a big wedding, do you?'

'Wedding?' She felt the colour drain from her face. From being in control, driving the situation, she was suddenly way behind. She'd offered a solution, but she hadn't been thinking as far ahead as a wedding.

'You wanted to know if I was asking you to marry me. If the choice is you or the advertisement, I'll take you.' As a proposal it lacked just about everything. Except the man she loved with all her heart. 'You *were* serious?'

She tried to say yes, but nothing came out as her voice momentarily stuck in her throat somewhere. She cleared it. 'Yes. I was serious.'

'Then I see no point in waiting. I'm free on Tuesday morning, if that suits you?'

Jane had a fleeting vision of candlelight, red roses, a diamond ring. The perfect proposal, followed by the perfect wedding, with the long white dress and orange blossom by the cartload. There'd be a posse of little bridesmaids and her entire family watching in stunned amazement as her father walked her up the aisle to give her away to the man of her dreams. Of any woman's dreams. And then she let it all go. She'd look dreadful in white and the orange blossom would undoubtedly droop.

Mark had asked her to marry him. Sort of. How much more perfect could it get? And if his proposal lacked romance, well, that was the way she'd planned it. Common sense ruled.

'Tuesday will be fine,' she replied, as calmly as if they

were discussing a project meeting. 'Would you like me to handle the details?' *Please say no. That you'll do it...*

'If you would.'

'Do you want me to invite anyone? Colleagues? I imagine you'll want your family—'.

'Is that necessary?' he asked, a small frown creasing his forehead as he looked up. 'I'd rather not have any fuss.'

He didn't want his mother or his sister there? It meant that little to him? She hadn't expected romance, but a certain amount of ceremony was usual to mark even the most low-key of weddings. She swallowed her hurt, her pride. 'No, it's not necessary. We'll just need a couple of witnesses. I'll see to it,' she said quickly, before he could ask her to find two total strangers to perform this service. Their marriage might not be made in heaven—more like the local DIY shop—but it wasn't going to be some hole-and-corner affair.

He nodded. 'You'd better find a replacement for yourself at the same time.' He offered a slightly rueful smile. 'Pity about that, but no plan is ever perfect.'

'No.' It wasn't perfect by a long way. But it was a work in progress. Having achieved her initial objective, she would have all the time in the world to go back to the drawing board and work on the fine details of how to get him to fall in love with her. 'There's Patsy,' she suggested. He looked blank. 'The girl in the planning department who covered for me while I was on holiday?'

'I didn't notice.'

Of course he hadn't. She'd worked very hard to make sure her absence didn't inconvenience him in any way. 'Then she's definitely the one. I'll sort it out tomorrow.'

'Right.' His brows came together in a frown and he looked at her sharply, as if he suspected he'd missed something. Then he let it go and said, 'Is that it? If you've finished straightening out my life can we look at that Maybridge contract?'

He didn't wait for her answer, just crumpled up the advertisement she'd typed out for him, tossed it in the waste-paper basket and reached for a file.

Working around a busy three-year-old was hard work, and Mark, after yet another interruption when Shuli had needed her supper, said, 'Look, why don't we take a break? I'll put her to bed, then we can do a couple of hours in peace.'

'I've got a better idea,' Jane said. 'Why don't I look after Shuli and leave you to get on with those figures?'

'Would you?' He pushed his fingers through his thick dark hair, leaving it sticking up at the crown. Just as he had the first time she'd seen him. Harassed and struggling to cope with the mess life had tossed in his lap. It had taken all her self-control not to reach out and smooth it for him then.

She still had to fight the impulse.

It was quiet. Blissfully quiet. Uninterrupted, he'd swiftly finished the calculations and now he needed Jane. She'd had more than enough time to bathe one small child and put her to bed. He walked out into the hall and listened. Nothing. About to call her, he realised he might wake Shuli and instead went upstairs.

The door to the nursery was open and Jane was sitting on the bed, gently stroking Shuli's fair curls. His heart turned over at the sweet intimacy of the scene. Jane was right. This was what his little girl needed more than anything.

Relief at how easy it had been with her here warred with guilt that he found it so difficult to cope with his own child. Relief won hands down. The thought of Jane taking care of things at home far outweighed the inconvenience of losing her in the office, and he suddenly felt as if a huge burden had been lifted from his shoulders.

Seeing him in the doorway, she put her finger to her lips,

set the listening device and then joined him, pulling the door partly closed behind her.

'You make it look so easy,' he said.

'I've had a lot of practise. I've got half a dozen nephews and nieces.' She had a family? He hadn't thought of that. 'You must be hungry. Shall we have something to eat now?' she asked. 'Or do you want to get straight back to work?'

'Let's eat. I'll get something sent in.' He headed for the stairs. 'What do you like?'

'Why don't I just make something quick? Some pasta or eggs?'

He glanced at her. 'You cook, too?'

'You're a very lucky man, Mark. I have an old-fashioned mother. She taught us all the basics.'

It occurred to him that he knew nothing of her background, her interests. He hadn't even asked her where she'd gone on holiday. For the past three years he'd used work to fill the emotional vacuum inside him. He'd cut himself off from everything human, vital. The only time he seemed to speak to his family these days was when he needed help with childcare. But he wasn't totally beyond redemption. 'How will she react to this wedding?'

'My mother? With considerable surprise, I imagine. Having given birth to four swans, she despaired of her little ugly duckling ever finding a mate.'

'You're kidding?'

Her eyes sparkled back at him. Of course she was.

'Why are you doing this, Jane? I can see the advantages from my point of view, but you're young. You have your life ahead of you. You should be looking for a man who can give you...' All of himself. That was what he'd been going to say. Her brows quirked up as he faltered. 'A little bit of romance,' he finished lamely.

'The girls in the office live for romance. As far as I can see it involves a great deal of weeping in the cloakroom followed by the consumption of chocolate in industrial quantities. It looks messy. Not to say a dietary nightmare.'

'Don't underrate it.'

'I don't underrate love,' she conceded, and a momentary sadness darkened her eyes. Then she shrugged. 'I just don't believe it's something you're likely to find in a club on a Saturday night.'

That was it, then. Her heart had been broken too. They'd make a perfect match. Even so... 'Will you promise me something?' She regarded him curiously from a pair of the darkest brown eyes, solemn now as she waited for him to continue. 'If you ever do fall in love—the real thing, one hundred per cent, no holds barred love—you must tell me. I wouldn't expect you to stay.'

Jane knew he was talking about the way it had been for him, with Caroline. She'd been treated to all the office gossip when she'd first joined the firm, heard how their marriage had been the perfect once-in-a-lifetime romance. How his wife's tragic death had nearly destroyed Mark, too.

And, despite her denial of a romantic nature, like the girls in the office she'd done her share of weeping. For him. And for herself. At home, in the privacy of her own bedroom. But this wasn't the moment to tell him that he was all the romance she'd ever need. Neither was it the moment to tell him that, like her mother, she was an old-fashioned girl who believed in taking her marriage vows seriously. Till death us do part.

'Jane?' he prompted, reaching out as if to keep her at his side, his hand beneath her arm, his look deeply intense.

'I promise,' she said.

'Thank you.'

And then she saw that in giving this promise she'd in some way absolved him from guilt about marrying her for his own selfish motives. Since her intention was to make his life easier, she tried to disregard the small stab of pain this caused, simply to be grateful that he hadn't thought to give her a similar promise from himself.

'Maybe you'd like to look around while you're up here,' he suggested brightly, shattering the quiet intimacy of the moment. 'You might like to have the suite overlooking the garden,' he added, opening a door and then standing back so that she could pass him and look around. 'Caroline designed it for guests and it's got pretty much everything.'

She was about to laugh and say that there was no need to take 'platonic' that far, when some inner sense of self-preservation warned her to hold her tongue. She already knew she'd have to wait for his heart. It seemed she'd have to wait for everything else, too.

# CHAPTER THREE

'YOU'VE done what?'

Jane, curled up on her best friend's sofa, with a mug of tea clutched comfortingly between her hands, repeated her news. 'I've asked Mark Hilliard to marry me.' She lifted her shoulders, bunching them against her neck. This was harder than the actual deed. 'At least, I manoeuvred him into a position where he asked me, which is much the same thing.'

'How?' she demanded. 'I could use some help in levering Greg into a proposal.' Then she grinned. 'You're a dark horse, Janey. I knew you were potty about the man, but I didn't know things had progressed to hand-holding over the desk. Your mother must be over the moon—'

'She doesn't know. The ceremony is going to be on Tuesday at the register office. Just the two of us and a couple of witnesses. That's why I'm here. To ask if you and Greg will be our witnesses.'

'Are you out of your mind? Your mum expects these things to be done properly. The full fairy tale bit. Bells, choir, a three-tier cake and enough champagne to launch the *QE2*—'

'Yes, well, this isn't exactly a fairy tale wedding. Which is why I'm not telling them until Wednesday.'

'She'll kill you. No, she'll think you're pregnant and she'll send your father to kill him...' She stopped. 'Ohmigod! You are pregnant!'

Jane's hands were shaking so much with delayed reaction that she put down her mug before she slopped tea over the sofa. Her voice was steady enough though, even if her smile was wry. 'One step at a time, Laine. One step at a time. He has to kiss me first.'

'Actually that's not true…' Then, as the penny dropped, 'Oh, crumbs, Janey, I hope you know what you're doing.'

Did she? This morning she'd been absolutely certain, but suppose she was still in the guest suite when they were celebrating their silver wedding? Suppose he never saw her as anything other than 'good old Jane'?

'Janey?' Laine prompted, seeking reassurance.

'Mark doesn't want any fuss and neither do I,' she said, choosing to answer her concerns about the wedding arrangements rather than her concern about the marriage. 'Let's face it, Laine, I was never cut out to play the beautiful blushing bride.' But she crossed her fingers before she said, 'Trust me. It's my wedding and I know what I'm doing.'

There was a pause while Laine digested this statement. 'Well, you usually do, I'll grant you that,' she conceded eventually.

'I get the man I love, a darling little girl…'

'Do you? Get him?'

'I'm working on it.'

'Marriage is enough of a gamble even when you're head over heels.'

'Rather less so when both parties have so much to gain and know exactly what they're getting. There are none of those untidy emotions to mess things up.'

'I'm sure fate will find some way to throw a spanner in the works. The ghost of his first wife, for instance. You'll always be in her shadow.' When Jane didn't answer, Laine pushed harder. 'Wasn't she a famous beauty? One of the ''girls in pearls''? A perfect English Rose?'

While Jane was pure Celt. Dark-haired, dark-eyed, and struggling to make five foot three in her outdoor shoes. 'I'll have to get busy with the pruning shears, then, won't I?'

Laine didn't laugh. 'Well, if it's what you want, then of

course Greg and I will be your witnesses.' She waited, apparently expecting some response. 'It is what you want?'

'I love him, Laine.'

'I see.' She didn't respond with the obvious question—does he love you? Which suggested she did see. Only too clearly. But then Laine could read a three-volume novel from a tone of voice. 'So, Mark Hilliard gets a live-in nanny and a housekeeper. What do you get out of it?'

'To be needed.'

'Don't underrate yourself. You're worth more than that.'

Jane was getting a little tired of the word 'underrate'. She was underrating nothing, least of all herself. 'At ten o'clock this morning nothing was further from Mark's mind than getting married. By eleven o'clock he'd set the date.' She kinked an eyebrow at her friend. 'Just who is underrating whom, here?'

Laine regarded her thoughtfully for a moment, then she laughed. 'Right. So why are we drinking tea? Let's celebrate!' Then, as she took a bottle of wine from the fridge, 'Please, please, please can I help you shop for "bad girl" underwear?'

'I think the situation calls for subtlety rather than a sledgehammer.'

'Silk French knickers are subtle. Satin camisoles are subtle.' Then, 'You've got this all worked out, haven't you?'

'Down to the last detail,' she said. 'I've even got my mother sorted. She'll be so delighted to get her youngest daughter off the shelf that she'll happily forgo the fancy wedding.'

Laine grinned. 'You can hope.'

'No, honestly,' she said, her face deadpan. 'And if you'd ever seen my dad's reaction to the announcement that yet another daughter was getting married, heard his pitiful pleas for her to elope, you'd understand that I'm doing them a kindness.'

'Your dad didn't mean it.'

'No?' Then she grinned, too. 'And I always thought he was serious. Oh, dear. But it'll be too late by then.'

'I wouldn't be in your shoes when your mother finds out. You'll have to flee the country. Go on an extended honeymoon until the dust settles…' Laine glanced at her. 'Is there going to be a honeymoon?'

'Not until the design contract for the Maybridge Arts Centre is signed. Maybe my parents could go away instead? They could console themselves with a luxury cruise on the money I'm saving them.' She took the glass of wine. 'I do have one problem, though. What am I going to wear on Tuesday?'

'Something elegant.'

'But simple.' She didn't want to turn up in some fancy outfit that would startle Mark. He saw the occasion as nothing more exciting than taking an hour out of the office to marry his plain, comfortable Jane; if she turned up in 'bride' clothes he'd probably take one look and run a mile.

But even with just a couple of witnesses it had to look like a wedding, feel like a wedding. He needed to be reminded that this wasn't just some job promotion with 'living in' privileges. The ceremony might be little more than a pared-to-the-bone formality, but they were both going to be making some solemn vows on Tuesday morning.

He was taking her as his wife.

Whatever anyone else might think, she wanted Mark left in no doubt about that.

'I'm sorry I had to bother you with that, Mark,' Jane said, as they left the register office. 'I should have realised you'd have to sign the form personally.'

'It's not a bother. We'd have had to go into town anyway. The banks want your signatures for the accounts you'll need—credit cards, that sort of thing.'

'Accounts?'

'Personal, housekeeping.'

'Oh.'

'You won't be working, so I thought if I gave you the same allowance as your salary? If you need more—'

'No! No,' she repeated, her nails digging into the palms of her hands. She hadn't given much thought to what she'd do for personal money, but it had never occurred to her that he'd just keep paying her a salary. But why not? That was the way he saw her. Laine was right. This was a mistake. 'Mark—'

'And you're going to need a ring.'

Her heart turned over. 'A ring?'

'A wedding ring.' She bit on her lip, fighting an overwhelming urge to weep with joy. All morning he'd been distant, absolutely businesslike, and her heart had been shrivelling up inside her. Suddenly the world felt wonderful. 'We might as well get it now,' he said, matter-of-factly. It didn't matter. He'd been thinking about it.

'Wedding rings?' The jeweller beamed. 'Congratulations.'

'Thank you,' Jane said quickly, when Mark looked slightly bemused.

'What are you looking for? Something classic in gold? Or platinum's very fashionable now,' the man said. 'And there seems to be something of a trend towards wedding rings set with precious stones.'

Mark turned to her. 'Choose whatever you want, Jane,' he said, apparently under the impression that it had nothing whatever to do with him.

'A wedding ring shouldn't be a fashion statement. It should be practical. It has to take a lot of hard knocks.' She smiled at the man. One of them should be smiling. 'I want something in gold, absolutely plain, not too wide.' Her finger was measured and then she was brought a selection of rings to look at. It wasn't difficult to choose. 'This one,' she said, picking out the kind of ring a woman could live with for a lifetime. She realised the jeweller was waiting for her to try it on and rather self-consciously slipped it onto her finger. 'Yes, it's fine. Mark?'

She expected him to nod and reach for his credit card. Instead he reached for her hand, holding it so that her fingers were stretched across his palm, and looked at it for what seemed a lifetime.

It was the nearest he'd come in the two and a half years she'd known him to an intimate gesture.

Did this count as 'hand-holding'?

His long, elegant, fingers, vibrant and warm against hers, seemed to spark a chain reaction of warmth that raced through her body, just as it had a thousand times in her imagination. Her imagination had been light years from reality.

Oh, yes. This was hand-holding on an epic scale.

'You're absolutely sure?' he asked, finally looking up at her.

As her hand began to tremble, betraying her calm exterior for the act it was, she snatched it back, pretending to take a closer look at the ring.

His touch had meant nothing; she must read nothing into it. He was simply concerned that she was choosing the plainest ring in the tray out of some misplaced reticence.

Utility wife, utility ring.

She reassured him. 'Mark, this is the ring I'd choose if I were marrying the Sultan of Zanzibar.'

He continued to regard her with his steady grey eyes. 'Are you telling me I've got competition?'

'Absolutely,' she replied, matching his serious expression. 'He calls me day and night, begging me to join his harem.'

'Is that right? Well, next time he calls, tell him you're spoken for.' He turned to the jeweller with a smile. 'That was surprisingly easy.'

'The young lady certainly seems to know her own mind.

A classic choice, if I may say so. Now, if I can just check your size, sir, I'll bring a matching ring for you to try.'

'Oh, but—'

Jane felt rather than saw Mark's small instinctive gesture as he curled his fingers, lifting his hand back no more than an inch. It was enough for her to see that he was still wearing the ring that Caroline had placed there.

'There's no time right now, Mark,' she said quickly. 'We have to get to the bank.' It was the first thing that came into her head. That and regret that she hadn't kept to her original plan to tell him that she wanted to wear her great-grandmother's ring. This was exactly the kind of situation she'd been hoping to avoid. She wanted everything to go as smoothly as possible. She didn't want him jerked into painful reminders at every turn. But she'd been betrayed by the need to be noticed, recognised. By her singing pleasure that he'd been thinking about her. 'And Shuli will be getting hungry.'

Once outside, he stopped and said, 'I'm sorry, Jane.' She covered his left hand briefly with her own in a wordless gesture of comfort. She could not bring herself to say that it didn't matter.

It did.

Back in the office, she ensured that her replacement was coping and then collected Shuli from the care of a curious receptionist so that everyone could work in peace.

'Is it true that you're leaving?'

With Patsy installed at her desk, already busy organising her own replacement, she could hardly deny it. Why would she want to deny it? 'Yes, it's true. Patsy's taking over from today, although I'll be in and out for the rest of the week,' she said, fastening the little girl into her pushchair.

'It's a bit sudden, isn't it? There's a wild rumour going around that you're marrying Mark Hilliard.' She said it as if it had to be some kind of joke, but Jane wasn't in the mood to be patronised, and since Mark had already informed his doubtless much relieved partners of the imminent improvement in his domestic situation it was scarcely a secret.

'Is there? Well, even a wild rumour has to be right once in a blue moon,' she said. And came close to adding that the speed of the wedding was due entirely to the fact that she was pregnant. With triplets.

She restrained herself in the sure and certain knowledge that the rumour machine was already way ahead of her with that one. Instead she contented herself with a smile, adding, 'If anyone is looking for me, I'm taking Shuli shopping for something totally gorgeous to wear for the occasion.' She didn't say which of them the 'totally gorgeous' something was for.

Mark returned to his office, but couldn't concentrate on work. Instead he sat at his desk, turning the wedding ring round and round on his finger. It was so much a part of him that it hadn't occurred to him that he would be expected to wear a new one. It did occur to him that he wasn't thinking about anything very much except his own feelings.

Jane had covered for him when he'd instinctively recoiled from the thought of a new ring. She had reached out to him offering instant reassurance rather than the reproach he'd deserved. The warmth of her touch still lingered comfortingly against his skin.

Only her eyes, huge and brown, had momentarily betrayed her hurt at his thoughtlessness.

He took one last look at the ring before slipping it from his finger, then, uncertain what to do with it, he tucked it away in his wallet before reaching for the intercom. 'Penny?' No, that wasn't right. 'Pansy?'

'Try Patsy,' a disembodied voice advised.

'Patsy. Of course. Sorry. I have to go out for half an hour. Can you ring round and put back the weekly progress meeting?'

'No problem. Everyone will understand.' Then, 'Look, I don't know if I did the right thing, but I've made a provisional booking at the Waterside for lunch on Tuesday.'

About to ask why she'd thought that necessary, he just managed to stop himself in time. 'Did Jane ask you to do that?'

'No, I used my own initiative. She said you'd want me to.' After another pause, 'If you've made other plans I can cancel, but Jane said you weren't going away. I thought you might like to surprise her.'

'And your initiative suggested lunch at the Waterside would be a suitable surprise?'

'Absolutely. If I'd just been swept off my feet with a whirlwind wedding I'd want a romantic lunch somewhere quiet by the river. Well, short of Paris in the spring.'

Paris? Jane wouldn't. expect to be taken away, would she? He tried to imagine walking along the banks of the Seine at night with Jane. The picture wouldn't come into focus. 'Paris will have to wait until we've signed the Maybridge contract, I'm afraid. And when you confirm the reservation at the Waterside make sure they've got a highchair, will you?'

'Is Shuli going to be a bridesmaid? How sweet. Do you want me to organise flowers?'

Rings, flowers, bridesmaids. What had happened to the simple no-nonsense ceremony he'd envisaged? He recalled the uneasy feeling he'd had that it couldn't be that easy. And wondered what else he'd overlooked.

As he tensed his hand he could still feel the ring that until a few minutes ago had been part of him. Could still see the mark, feel the weight of it.

Could still feel the warmth of Jane's reassuring touch.

Then, realising that Patsy was still waiting, he said, 'No. Thank you. I'd rather organise the flowers myself. I'll be out of the office for about half an hour.'

Choosing the flowers was a pleasure, he discovered, un-

til, opening his wallet to get out his charge card, he saw
the wedding ring glinting in its depths. It brought back the
flash of hurt in Jane's eyes and he tried to imagine how
she'd feel if she ever saw the ring. Or found it in the back
of a drawer.

He didn't want, ever, to make her look like that again.
She deserved his total loyalty.

Which was why, on his way back to the office, he took
a detour by the river and dropped the ring into the deep-
est part.

# CHAPTER FOUR

MARK was waiting on the steps of the Town Hall, the white rosebud in his buttonhole drawing indulgent glances from people passing in and out of the building. Shuli, wearing her new dress, a ribbon-tied posy clutched in her chubby hand, was fidgeting at his side. He was looking at his watch.

'I told you we shouldn't be late,' Jane said, as the taxi came to halt.

'Nonsense,' Laine declared. 'You have to give a man time to look into the void. Consider what life would be like if you didn't turn up. You're Miss Cool. You know that.'

She knew nothing. She'd spent the night looking into her own dark void, considering what life would be like if she'd got it wrong. Then this morning the florist had arrived with a spray of rosebuds and white freesias arranged in a silver Victorian flower holder, with a card from Mark that simply said 'Thank you.' And her cool façade had been washed away on a hot tide of tears.

It had taken a ton of concealer to cover the black rings and blotchy skin before Laine had arrived to put the finishing touches, help her with her hair. Help her dress in the fine cashmere *shalwar kameez* that had cost a month's salary.

Laine had whisked her to the boutique and wouldn't let her leave until she'd bought it. 'It's a wonderful compromise. Really special, but you'll be able to wear it anywhere...'

Now, after adjusting the long chiffon silk scarf Jane had wound once around her neck, leaving the long tails to trail behind her in the merest suggestion of a bridal veil, Laine handed her the spray of flowers and said, 'Well, what are you waiting for? He'll take one look and won't believe just how clever he's been.'

Was 'clever' going to be enough? Stepping out of the taxi, Jane couldn't quite meet Mark's eyes, afraid of what she might see there. Or rather not see there. Instead she swooped to gather the little girl into her arms. 'Darling, don't you look just good enough to eat!'

'You're supposed to say that to the groom, Jane.' Laine offered her hand to Mark, introduced herself. 'I'm Jane's best woman. We've been friends since nursery school.' She turned to the man behind her. 'And this is Greg,' she said, linking her arm with his. 'He's my best man and I'm hoping he'll be sufficiently inspired by today's simple and painless ceremony to follow your great example to pusillanimous men everywhere.'

'Sorry, Laine, but I don't think I can help you there. My heart is as faint as the next man's.'

Jane, already a bundle of nerves, thought she was the one who'd faint. He'd got cold feet. Decided this was all a huge mistake. She'd have to leave the town. The county. Possibly the country.

'It seems to be taking all my time to remember to breathe,' he said. 'Inspiration is quite beyond me. It's all Jane's fault.' Putting Shuli down before she dropped her, Jane looked up sharply. 'I've spent the last five minutes convinced that you'd changed your mind.'

'I wouldn't leave you standing here, Mark,' she said, hurt that he'd believe her capable of such cruelty.

Laine, behind him, lifted one expressive brow, then said, 'The traffic was terrible.'

This was a nightmare. So stiff, so formal. 'Thank you for the flowers…' Jane's voice failed her, dying away to leave an awkward silence.

'Look, I don't want to rush you two,' Greg said, coming

to the rescue, 'but I think that's the next wedding party arriving.'

Jane turned and saw two young people surrounded by friends, all of them laughing, happy.

'Are you ready?' Mark asked. And she nodded, her throat too stuffed with what felt like hot rocks to speak. Would she be able to say her vows? Would nodding count?

'She's ready,' Laine said, taking Shuli's hand and leading the way, turning back to add flippantly, 'I just hope you haven't forgotten the rings.'

Jane flinched and, looking anywhere but at the man she was about to marry, she blinked back a tear. Laine was right. It wasn't supposed to be like this.

If anyone had asked him to describe Jane Carmichael, Mark knew he would have been pressed to say much more than that she was a plain little thing. That the black suits she habitually wore never quite seemed right and she fought a constant battle to control a mass of hair that was neither black nor properly brown. That she had kind eyes. Smiled easily. Was comfortable to be with.

Her arrival outside the Town Hall had shattered that image of her.

'...I, Mark Edward Hilliard, take you, Jane Louise Carmichael...' Jane listened to his low, steady voice as he made the solemn vow. Then it was her turn to repeat the words after the registrar.

'...I, Jane Louise Carmichael...' Her voice had never seemed so faint, but she made it through without a mistake.

The registrar smiled at Mark. 'Do you have the rings?'

He produced the ring she'd chosen from his pocket and placed it on her finger, again repeating the solemn words. But when she would have turned back to the registrar he opened his hand. Lying in his palm was another ring, bright and new as the one he'd just placed on her own finger. A matching pair.

Only then did she realise that his left hand was bare, with just a lighter band of skin to show where another ring had once been.

The registrar, noticing nothing odd, prompted her promise. But her fingers were shaking as she took the ring and placed it on his finger. Her voice was shaking, too, as she made her promise. Had he thought of the meaning as he'd said his vows?

'You may kiss the bride.'

The momentary hesitation before he brushed his lips lightly against her own answered that particular question.

'Daddy!' He looked down at Shuli. 'Can I have a baby brother now?'

'Shh! Not now, sweetie,' Jane said, scooping her up to distract her while Mark signed the register. Then she did the same, her signature shakier than usual.

'Would you like to join us for lunch?' Mark asked Laine and Greg as they all left the registrar's office. 'I've got a table at the Waterside.'

Jane turned, astonished, to look up at him. 'The Waterside? When did you organise that?'

'I didn't. It was Patsy's idea. She was practising using her initiative.'

'Really? I didn't think she was *that* good,' she joked. Joked! Inside, she was shrivelling up at the make-believe of a romantic lunch together, and she turned to Laine. 'Of course you must come.'

Her friend, apparently reading the panic signal loud and clear, said, 'Try and stop us.'

'She arranged a car, too.' Mark offered a half-smile. 'Maybe she thought I'd be too nervous to drive myself.'

'Maybe she thought you'd be swimming in champagne,' Greg suggested.

'If that's the case I imagine it's already on ice.'

'Well, I sincerely hope so,' Laine said. 'This is Jane's big day.'

'I wonder if you'd go and see if the driver is there?' he asked, without comment. 'I said to come back at twelve. And could you take Shuli with you? We'll be along in a minute.'

'It'll be back to normal tomorrow,' Jane said quickly as he turned to her.

'I do hope not. "Normal" has been a nightmare.'

'Not any more.'

'No.'

She waited.

'I just wanted to tell you how lovely you look. I've never seen your hair loose before.'

She didn't wear it loose very often. It took an entire bottle of conditioner to tame it. But for today she'd made the effort, catching it at her nape with an ebony clasp and leaving it to hang down her back. 'It would be a nuisance in the office.'

'That won't be a problem any more.' He lifted her hand, looked at the ring he'd so recently placed on her finger. 'It looks a bit lonely all by itself, don't you think?' But he clearly didn't expect an answer because he reached into his jacket pocket and, spreading her fingers, slipped another ring beside the gold band.

The diamonds flashed back at her in the sunlight. Three considerable diamonds that had been set gypsy-style, almost flush in the gold. 'I'm sure the Sultan of Zanzibar would have given you a diamond as big as a paperweight. But, since you won't be sitting in a harem with nothing to do but your nails, I thought this would be more…practical.'

'They're industrial diamonds?' His head came up sharply and her hand flew to her mouth. 'No—sorry. Please forget I said that. It's nerves.'

'Nerves?' He looked astonished. 'I don't believe it. I've never seen anyone looking less flustered.'

'That's because I'm numb with terror.' Then, realising that it probably wasn't the most tactful thing she could have said, she rushed on. 'I was sure I'd make a total hash of it. Get my name wrong. Get *your* name wrong.' She was babbling. Big breath. Look at the ring. Say something sensible. Except how could she be cool and sensible when he'd just given her the most perfect, most exquisite ring? That was it. Thank him for the ring.

'The ring is beautiful, Mark. Absolutely, incredibly, wonderfully…practical.' She blinked back a tear. 'Thank you.'

'I'm glad you like it.'

Like it? If he'd read her mind he couldn't have chosen anything she'd like more, but she mustn't cry. It would embarrass him terribly.

If she concentrated really hard on the hideous mess it would make of all Laine's careful make-up, she'd get through it.

'I love it.' The nearest she could come to saying I love you. Oh, hell! Think of something else. Anything else. 'But I have a confession to make.' He waited for her to go on. 'I lied about the Sultan.'

'You mean he doesn't phone you day and night?' Mark didn't sound totally surprised.

'Actually he was deposed in 1964.'

'Well, I'm glad you told me,' he said, then added solemnly, 'I was afraid I'd have to let you down gently, warn you that someone was pulling your leg.' Only the small creases at the corners of his eyes suggested that, while somewhat under-used in recent years, Mark's GSOH was still in good working order. 'Shall we move, before Laine and Greg think we've ducked out of buying them lunch?'

Patsy had let her romantic nature run away with her and rented a limousine for the day, so there was plenty of room for the five of them. As Mark was distracted by Shuli's insistence on climbing onto his lap, Laine raised a querying eyebrow.

Jane just wiggled her fingers in reply and waited for Laine's jaw to drop. Her friend obliged and clearly couldn't wait to get her alone in the powder room at the Waterside in order to demand a full account of what had just happened.

She had to wait. They walked into the intimate little reception bar of the restaurant to be greeted by a loud cheer. Mark's partners and all their staff were there before them, presents piled high, champagne standing by, eager to wish them every happiness.

'I should have guessed,' Jane murmured to Laine as all the girls surged round her to look at the ring, all the men to kiss the bride. 'I *knew* Patsy couldn't have done all this without someone authorising it.'

'Mark?'

'No, one of his partners…' For a moment she'd thought it might have been him…hoped it might have been. But when she'd turned to look up at him, it had been obvious he was as surprised as she was. 'This is Charlie Young's idea, I imagine.'

By way of confirmation the man himself called for order. 'Jane, Mark—I know you both thought you were going to have a quiet romantic lunch together and are probably horrified to discover you're going to be sharing your special day with this unruly bunch. But we couldn't let the moment pass without letting you know how happy we are for you both.' There was a hum of approval. 'And maybe pick up a few hints on how to keep an office romance that quiet.' Amidst the laughter, he raised his glass. 'To Jane and Mark.'

'To Jane and Mark.'

Then someone called out, 'Well, go on, Mark, give her a kiss.'

Beside her Jane felt him tense, and instinctively she

reached for his hand. One thing to kiss her at the register office, witnessed by strangers. Quite another in front of people who knew them both. Who'd known Caroline.

For a moment he gripped her fingers, then he turned to her and, with his eyes fixed upon hers, lifted her hand to his lips. And the only sound in the room was a soft sigh from the women.

The party broke up just after four, when an exhausted Shuli dropped asleep on Mark's shoulder.

He leaned back against the soft leather upholstery of the limousine and said, 'That was surprisingly good fun.'

'Yes, it was kind of them. I'll write thank-you notes to Charlie and everyone for the presents tomorrow.'

'Totally efficient as always?'

She turned sharply, but he was teasing. 'Not totally efficient. That would suggest I'd discovered some way of telling my mother about today and surviving.'

He looked perplexed. 'You didn't tell your mother that you were getting married?'

'Did you tell yours?'

'Well, no. But she's at an environmental conference in New York. And Portia's deeply involved in some legal wrangle at the European Parliament.'

And it wasn't as if he was marrying a glittering society beauty this time round. Just good old platonic Jane. Nothing to get excited about.

'It's a pity they don't make cards,' Jane said.

He frowned. 'Cards?'

'Greetings cards. ''Just to let you know that blank and blank were married on the blank.'''

'Maybe they do.' Then, when she gave him an old-fashioned look, 'No, I don't suppose there's much call for that sort of thing. Do you want me to ring her? Explain—?'

'No!' Explanations were the last thing she wanted.

'Explain why we didn't wait and do the whole banns and church bit,' he finished gently. 'Because of Shuli.'

And have her mother speculate on whether she'd married for Mark's convenience rather than her own? Besides, that wasn't why they'd opted for the fast-track wedding and he knew it. 'No,' she said. 'Really. I can handle it. But not until tomorrow.'

The evening, which she'd been so certain would be full of awkward moments, passed in a whirl of Shuli's needs. Exhausted, it was a relief for Jane to stretch out beside the child, cuddling up to her as she read her a long fairy story. She was in no hurry to go downstairs and face reality.

Shuli had been insistent that Jane bath her, so Mark had changed into a pair of comfortable chinos and a polo shirt, opened a bottle of wine, looked at the labels on the wedding presents and eventually, when he'd been able to wait no longer, had gone to look for her.

He found her, fast asleep and curled up beside Shuli, looking like a child herself in soft grey sweats. He picked up the book she'd been reading, put it on the night table. Then he carefully picked up Jane and carried her to the guest room, removing her shoes before covering her up, the way he'd done for Shuli more times than he could remember.

She didn't stir. Probably hadn't slept a wink the night before. Well, neither had he. But he was used to it.

He drew the curtains, then lingered, not wanting to leave, reliving that astonishing moment when his lips had touched hers. It had been the barest touch and yet, like the touch of her hand against his in the jeweller's, the heat lingered. And on an impulse he bent to kiss her again.

# CHAPTER FIVE

JANE woke with a start and sat up in the dense dark, not knowing where she was. Then it all came back to her with a rush. The wedding, the reception, the champagne. The guest room.

She fell back against the pillow. Then she sat up again as it occurred to her that maybe Shuli had cried out, her sleep disturbed by too much excitement. She hadn't been plied with champagne, but she had eaten an awful lot of ice cream.

She reached for the bedside lamp, missed and knocked it flying. 'Oh, sugar…' If the child wasn't already awake she soon would be. She crawled about on the floor until she found the lamp, then switched it on. That was when she realised she was still wearing the clothes she'd changed into before she'd bathed Shuli.

She sat back on her heels and frowned. The last thing she could remember was reading Shuli a bedtime story. The combination of a sleepless night, stress and vintage fizz had clearly knocked her out as effectively as a sleeping pill. She had the headache to prove it.

Great start. So much for totally efficient, totally in control Jane Carmichael.

The light caught the diamonds on her hand and they flashed a reminder that it wasn't only the calm and order that were things of the past. She was no longer Jane Carmichael, but Mrs Mark Hilliard.

She gave a little shiver, not from cold, but apprehension. The word 'home' had come naturally to her thoughts, yet as she put the lamp back on the table and looked around the exquisite suite she knew she could never call it that. Not while she stayed in the guest room.

This was Caroline's house: every perfect inch of it. She'd chosen the furniture, the wallpaper, the colour of the paint. There were even some of her clothes, still in dry cleaners' bags, hanging in the guest room wardrobe where someone had put them, out of the way.

She was here on the sufferance of a ghost. Feeling suffocated, choked, she pulled back the curtains to breathe in the sweet fresh air pouring in at the window.

The sky was the pearlescent grey of the pre-dawn, and she glanced at her watch to check the time. Not quite five. She'd heard no sound from Shuli, but she checked anyway. Anything to get out of that room. The child was fast asleep, her curls a tumbled halo on her pillow.

It must have been her own uneasy thoughts that had disturbed her, then.

She'd allowed Laine to believe that she had everything under control, that marriage had simply been the first step in her master plan. Ha! Some plan.

Here she was on the first morning of her married life, alone in the guest suite and still wearing the clothes she'd changed into when she'd gone to bath Shuli. It had been her wedding night, and the seductive nightgown that had been Laine's gift was still packed up in a suitcase somewhere; the only clothes she'd shed had been her shoes.

That was no way to set about reminding a man that he was made of flesh and blood. No way to infiltrate herself into his mind, exorcise the past.

Not that she'd have lingered on the landing to flash a bare shoulder as Mark followed her up the stairs—Laine's parting suggestion. Like the bad-girl underwear, it just wasn't her.

No, she'd had it all worked out. She was going to be the perfect wife, taking the strain, easing the burden. And hopefully reminding him that he could still laugh. And, starting

as she meant to go on, she'd stocked the fridge in readiness
to cook a perfect wedding-night supper.

Talk about falling asleep on the job!

But now, at five in the morning, her alter ego was wide
awake and whispering sedition, suggesting that *he'd* got it
made, but questioning what was in this marriage for her.

Confused, but certain that she wasn't going to get any
more sleep, she decided to go downstairs and make herself
a cup of tea.

Mark, used to sleeping with one ear listening for Shuli,
woke on full alert. It wasn't Shuli, but something had
woken him, and after a moment straining to identify any
unusual sound he heard a door being opened with infinite
care.

Jane. As he lay there, listening to her move quietly across
the hall to look in on the sleeping child, he felt an unexpected surge of pleasure in the realisation that he was no
longer on his own. That for the first time since he'd become
a father he had someone to share the responsibility, the
broken nights when she had a cold, the fear that he
wouldn't be good enough.

Someone who cared.

Not wanting her to think he was abandoning all responsibility for Shuli to her, he swung out of bed and headed
for the door. Then, realising that he probably needed to be
wearing more than a pair of boxers, he picked up a robe
and tied it about him.

He was too late. Shuli was fast asleep and Jane had returned to her own bed. Feeling oddly disappointed, he stood
for a little while watching his daughter. The source of so
much delight and so much pain. She was sleeping more
peacefully than he could recall in a long time.

He lifted the cover over her shoulder, gently kissed her
curly head and was returning to his room when he saw the

glow of a light spilling from the kitchen. Had Jane gone downstairs?

Concerned that she might be suffering from the after-effects of Charlie Young's boisterous hospitality, he went to see if she needed anything. And came to an abrupt halt as he turned at the foot of the stairs.

Jane was sitting at the breakfast island, her legs wrapped around a stool, dunking a teabag in a mug, her shadowy figure backlit by a single downlighter.

Her hair had exploded into a thick mass of waves and curls, while her mouth, far too large for her face and usually tucked up tidily into a smile, had drooped into a soft, pensive pout.

Yesterday, arriving for the wedding, he'd been startled at how different she looked out of the stark black suits she wore in the office. But this was a Jane he'd never even suspected existed. And as he stood there his body disturbingly reminded him that he was a man.

'Jane? Is anything wrong?' His voice came out more sharply than he'd intended and she jumped, sending the mug crashing on its side so that hot tea cascaded over the edge of the worktop onto her legs. Without thinking he rushed to grab her, pull her from the stool and away from the scalding liquid. 'Are you hurt?' he demanded. 'Get those things off...' He tugged at her jog-pants, pulling the wet fabric away from her skin, and discovered somewhat late in the day that her eyes could spit fire as easily as they smiled.

'What the hell do you think you're doing?'

Realising, belatedly, how his reaction to the drama could be misinterpreted, he released her. 'I was just trying to minimise the damage. You need to get out of those pants—'

'I know, but I'm not helpless.' She turned away from him and peeled down the jog-pants, kicking them off.

'And get them under cold water,' he added, heading for the fridge.

'I know that, too! I'm not a complete idiot.' She turned on the tap and, grabbing a towel, held it beneath the flow to soak it. 'I was a Girl Guide—'

'Turn round.'

She turned, but only to berate him further. 'I did first—' Her verbal onslaught came to an abrupt halt as he slowly and carefully poured the contents of the water container he'd taken from the fridge over the pink patches on her thighs. It was a big container and it was a long time before she could draw in sufficient breath to gasp out, 'That's enough! I'm fine… Please… Stop…'

He looked up. 'Sure?' She nodded wordlessly. 'How does it feel?'

'Totally numb. I think I'm in more danger of frostbite than blistering.'

He switched on the main light and took a closer look. Her legs were still pink but he suspected that she was right. It was from the cold water rather than the scald. He looked up. 'Fortunately the jog-pants saved you from any serious damage.'

Jane looked around; yes, well, he could quite understand why she wouldn't want to look at him. If anyone was an idiot it was him. Startling her that way—

'Whoever would have thought so little water would go such a long way?' she said. 'I'd better mop it up.' She lifted her shoulders in an awkward little shrug. 'If you'll tell me where the mop is.'

'Not a chance. You're going to sit down while I make you a fresh cup of tea.' Paddling through the iced water, he led her back to the stool, but, since her legs were already sparking libidinous ideas, he thought it wiser not to attempt to lift her onto it. 'And this time try not to throw it over yourself.'

'I did not do any such thing! You startled me!'

Lord, but she was jumpy. 'I was pulling your leg, Jane. For heaven's sake, relax.'

She looked as if she was about to tell him what he could do with his leg-pulling, too. Then she gave a little shiver. 'I'm sorry, Mark. I'm not usually so jumpy. And I'm sorry I shouted at you for trying to help.'

'Shout away. You had every right.' Her reaction had revealed a side of his unflappable secretary that he'd never witnessed before; it had been worth a scolding. 'I'm the one who should be apologising. I heard you come down and I thought you might be...' Sick. Or maybe just sleepless, lying awake and wondering how she could ever have made such a big mistake. The thought was enough to make him feel ill.

During the last few days he'd felt as if he was reaching light at the end of some long tunnel. He'd scarcely given a second thought to how she was feeling. After all, this had been her idea. She'd been pushing him to find someone, a partner, a mother for Shuli, and when it came right down to it there was no escaping the fact that she'd put the idea of marrying her into his head.

And he'd grabbed it with both hands.

Because it had been the easiest thing to do? An answer to all his prayers? When had he become so selfish? So self-centred? It was too late to suggest she think again. All he could do was make sure she never regretted her generous impulse. Do everything within his power to make her happy.

He realised she was still waiting for him to complete the sentence. 'I thought you might be worrying about how your mother will react the your news.'

'My mother, my father, my four big sisters and their husbands, as well as several dozen cousins. Oh, and a parcel of nieces who'll be furious that they didn't get to be bridesmaids,' she said. 'They are going to be really fed up.' Her answer was undoubtedly true, but had been seized on with such enthusiasm that he suspected he might have of-

fered an excuse that was a lot easier to admit to than the
truth.

'Maybe we should leave the country,' he suggested.

She finally smiled. 'Good plan. Unfortunately you've got
a tight deadline on the Maybridge project.'

'I know, but if your father's going to come after me with
shotgun—'

'Why would he do that? It isn't as if you've done me
wrong. This was all my idea...' She suddenly found it necessary to check on her legs.

'How are they?'

She looked up.

'Your legs?'

'Fine. That was quick thinking—if out of the cruel-to-
be-kind school of nursing. I bet you rip sticky plasters off
hairy limbs, too.'

'Is there another way?' Her legs, he realised, were not
just fine. They were very fine. Jane might not be tall, but
her legs left nothing to be desired: proportionately long,
shapely, with a pair of very fetching ankles. His treacherous
body found an ally in a mind quick to offer an alternative
occupation to tea-drinking for two newlyweds awake in the
early hours of the morning.

He couldn't understand it. His libido had lain dormant
for years. Last week, when they'd agreed that this was a
sensible, logical and totally platonic marriage, nothing had
been further from his mind than making love to his new
wife.

Certainly nothing had been further from hers or she'd
never have agreed to it. And he couldn't change the rules
now, just because he was unexpectedly aroused. He wasn't
that selfish. Realising that he was staring, he said, 'I thought
you were going to sit down while I made us both a cup of
tea.' It would occupy his hands.

Jane, feeling suddenly naked, was about to refuse, rush
away and cover herself up. But Mark didn't seem in the

least bit bothered by the fact that her sweat top barely covered her knickers. Not nearly bothered enough, if all he
could think of was making a cup of tea.

So much for Laine urging a little provocative shoulder
display. It didn't seem at all fair that a glimpse of his naked
chest could leave her feeling weak with lust, while her entire legs were apparently not worth a second glance.

Forget naked anything; she'd be wiser to stick to her first
plan. Which was why, eschewing modesty, she did what
any perfect wife would do under the circumstances. She
ignored the stool and instead found the mop for herself and
dried the floor. Then she cleaned up the mess made by the
tea.

'You didn't have to do that,' Mark said, carrying across
a couple of mugs of tea and sliding onto a stool beside her.
'A couple of people come in a van three times a week and
clean from top to bottom.'

To distract herself from the body heat leaping the small
space between them so that the tiny hairs on her thighs
stood on end, she said, 'Maybe we should cut their visits
back to once a week or I won't have anything to do.'

'Caroline never had any trouble filling her time. Upper
Haughton has a busy social life, apparently.'

'Do you mean there are a lot of coffee mornings, jumble
sales and other time-consuming ways of raising money for
worthy causes as an excuse for catching up with the gossip?'

'Don't forget the village fête.' He turned and looked
down at her, a wry smile pulling at the corners of his
mouth. 'You're right. It doesn't sound that exciting.'

'I might think that, but, since this is all new to me, I'll
reserve judgement.'

'Shuli will keep you on the run.'

'Undoubtedly. Does she go to a playgroup?'

'One of her nannies took her to something called Tiny
Tots at the village hall.' He turned away, his jaw tightening,

and suddenly found something of enormous interest in his mug. 'It was there that Shuli discovered other children didn't have nannies, they had mummies. That's when she started getting so difficult.'

Jane made a move to reach out, cover his hand with her own. He was so close. It would be so easy to offer that simple, wordless assurance that everything was going to be put right. That from this day forward he wouldn't have to worry about a thing.

He might not, but she was beginning to get an inkling of just how far out on an emotional limb she'd crawled. So she restrained herself, instead picking up the mug of tea and cradling it for a little personal comfort between her fingers. 'Well, she's got one now,' she said. 'I hope she won't be disappointed.'

'No.' He turned to her. 'I think she's been telling me for some time that she'd chosen you.'

She frowned.

'Think about it. Every time she played up and I had to bring her into the office she spent the day with you. She adores you, Jane. She hasn't stopped talking about you all weekend. I should have realised sooner, but I guess I just wasn't listening.'

Who would blame him? It was obvious that such a sacrifice would be above and beyond the call of duty unless desperation drove you to it. She put down the mug before she had another accident.

'She'll be waking up any minute. I'd better go and take a shower, see if I can find something to wear. I packed so quickly that it'll take me days to sort everything out.'

She slipped down from the stool and Mark watched her as she crossed the kitchen, vaguely troubled by his unexpected reaction to a woman he'd thought he knew so well. He knew what he was getting out of this marriage, but what had driven her to make such a choice? Not for the 'lovely home' or the 'comfortable life', he was certain. Or to avoid the tears and chocolate that went with conventional match-making. Had her heart been broken by some careless man too stupid to recognise what he'd got? Afraid of being hurt again, had she opted out and settled for friendship?

He promised himself that she wouldn't be sorry with her bargain. That he would be the best friend she'd ever had.

'I promise you,' she said, echoing his thoughts as she bent to pick up her tea-soaked jog-pants, 'I'm not in a habit of sleeping in the clothes I'm wearing.'

'That was entirely my fault. Maybe I should have woken you, but you looked so peaceful.'

'Woken me?' She straightened, slowly turned around. 'Peaceful?' She said the word as if it were unknown to her.

'You were reading to Shuli,' he said. 'Remember? It must have been one heck of a boring story because it put you both to sleep. I thought you'd be more comfortable in your own bed.' A deep flush flamed her cheeks. She was embarrassed? Because he'd picked her up and put her to bed? It wasn't as if he'd taken her to his. Or even undressed her. This probably wasn't the moment to admit that he'd kissed her goodnight. 'I thought I'd better take off your shoes, though. I hope you don't mind?'

She swallowed. 'Why should I mind?'

'You seem a little...disconcerted.' Then, 'Has anyone ever told you that you've got very pretty feet?' The desire to tease her, just a little, was a wicked temptation. But irresistible. He'd never seen a woman blush like that before.

'All the time,' she said, then added airily, 'People stop me in the street to remark on them.'

'And they say the British are a reserved people.' He shook his head, hiding a smile. 'I hadn't noticed how small they are. Your feet.' He hadn't been noticing much at all, he thought. Not for a long time.

Unable to shuffle them out of sight, hide the pretty pink toenails, she backed towards the door. 'I'd better take that shower.'

'Better make it a cool one.' Her eyes widened. 'Hot water will make your legs sting,' he explained. What the heck had she thought he meant?

'Oh, right. I'd forgotten all about them.' She took another step backwards. 'Great first aid.'

Mark watched her retreat all the way to the hall, where she gave up any pretence of dignity, and turned to bolt up the stairs.

He remained where he was for a long time, just smiling and thinking that this was a great way to start the day.

Then, hearing Shuli squealing with pleasure as Jane went to see if she was awake, he realised that it was time he thought about getting ready for work. And that he might benefit from taking his own advice regarding the temperature of his shower.

# CHAPTER SIX

MARK put his head around the nursery door. 'Jane, I've got an early meeting with the project team, so I'll get off now. I should be home by seven.'

Jane, who'd discovered that dressing a wriggling three-year-old who would much rather play took a lot longer than she'd anticipated, leapt to her feet. 'But what about breakfast?' The whole essential coffee, fresh orange juice, cereals and egg thing that every perfect wife provided for her man. That her mother had provided for her family without apparent effort every morning of her life. 'It's the most important meal of the day.'

Mark just grinned, picked up his daughter and kissed her. The dungarees fell off. 'I'm used to getting my own breakfast. And Shuli's too.' He turned to her, still holding his little girl. 'This morning has been a piece of cake.' For a moment she thought he was going to kiss her, too, but then he put Shuli down and said, 'If I'm going to be late I'll ring you. Bye, Shuli. Be good.'

'Be good,' Shuli called back.

'Take care,' Jane whispered. Then, when the sound of Mark's car had faded into the distance, she picked up the little pair of dungarees and started again.

Breakfast took an age. And then, on the dot of nine, two ladies arrived in a bright yellow van and set about dusting and polishing the house with frightening efficiency. They seemed to be everywhere, and Jane didn't need much tempting to leave the call to her mother for a quieter moment.

Besides, a walk would clear her head, give her time to

think through exactly what she'd say. Fastening Shuli into her buggy, she set off to explore the village.

Patsy put her head around the drawing office door. 'Mark, there's a personal call for you. Shall I put it through to you here?'

'Sure.' Anticipating Jane's voice, he tucked the phone against his shoulder and carried on hatching in an area to be detailed by a draughtsman. 'What's the problem?' he asked.

'I don't know, Mr Hilliard,' a woman's voice replied briskly. 'That's why I'm calling you. To get some answers.'

'Sorry?' He straightened. 'Who is this?'

'Jennifer Carmichael. Your mother-in-law?' she prompted.

The pencil point snapped as Mark pressed down too hard. 'Jane rang you.'

'No, Mr Hilliard, she did not. And since I have no way of contacting her to confirm the astonishing news that my youngest daughter was married yesterday, I'm calling you.'

'Mrs Carmichael—'

'Is it true?'

'Well, yes, but I really think—' He really thought she should be having this conversation with Jane, but Mrs Carmichael was not in the mood to listen to his thoughts.

'Is she pregnant?'

That at least he could answer. 'No…' Realising that twenty pairs of ears, having caught the name, were straining to hear what he had to say, he cut short the sentence. 'No,' he repeated firmly.

'Then maybe you can offer some other explanation as to why she chose to marry in what appears to be unseemly haste and without a single member of her family present?'

'She was going to call you this morning,' he hedged, wondering what on earth had happened to stop her. He was certain something had, because Jane wasn't the kind of woman to duck a difficult task, no matter how thorny. 'First thing,' he added.

'I'll talk to Jane later. Right now I'm asking you, Mr Hilliard.'

'Mark,' he said, inviting her to use his given name.

Jane's mother made no indication that she was prepared to make any concession to familiarity until she'd heard his explanation, but he wasn't about to tell her anything with an audience. 'I'm not in my office right now, Mrs Carmichael. May I call you back in a couple of minutes?'

'Please do.'

He didn't exactly race back to his office, taking the time to call home on his mobile and find out what Jane wanted him to say. He got the answering machine.

Mark arrived home minus the warm feeling with which he'd started the day. In fact he was in a mood to chew rocks. He'd been forced to cancel two meetings and leave a deputy to stand in at a third. In two and a half years as his secretary Jane had never let him down. They'd been married for one day and Miss Jekyll had suddenly turned into Mrs Hyde.

The side gate to the garden was locked, so he let himself in through the front door and immediately heard the sound of childish laughter coming from the kitchen. He felt a rush of relief and was forced to acknowledge that it wasn't just anger at having his day wrecked that had brought him home in the middle of the afternoon. Each time he'd phoned and got no answer his unease had increased. He'd been here before.

He stopped the thought. Clearly no disaster had befallen either of them.

Then, as he opened the kitchen door, he was forced to revise that conclusion. 'Disaster' might be overstating it, but Jane, looking as if she been dragged through a muddy pond by her hair, was down on her knees scrubbing at the tiles with a hard brush. Lying on an old blanket, his nose flat to the floor and looking decidedly sheepish, was a shaggy half-grown pup of doubtful parentage. Shuli, sitting high above the mess, fastened safely in her old high chair, was laughing delightedly.

'Daddy!' she cried, reaching out her chubby little arms to him.

Jane, up to her arms in hot soapsuds, shuddered. 'Not yet, sweetheart,' she said, looking up at the child. 'Not for hours. Please,' she added fervently.

Then, realising that Shuli wasn't looking at her, but at something or someone behind her, she turned and saw him. Six foot plus of elegant, three-piece-suited and perfectly groomed manhood standing in the kitchen doorway, looking as if he'd just been hit with a brick. Her heart, which was already struggling to maintain an optimistic beat, gave up the effort and hit her boots. 'Oh…sugar.'

'It's great to see you, too,' Mark said, crossing the kitchen to Shuli.

This was her worst nightmare. The dog. The mess. And Mark arriving home to find his beautiful home not the haven of peace he had anticipated, he'd bargained for, she'd promised, but in uproar.

It shouldn't have happened. It wouldn't have happened if he'd stuck to his usual routine. She'd never known him leave the office before six. She should have had plenty of time to clean up the house—and herself—and prepare the quiet, relaxed evening she'd planned. First some quality time, while Mark played with Shuli before bedtime. Then a drink while she was putting the last-minute touches to dinner. Only then had she planned to admit to the puppy. When he was in a relaxed and receptive mood.

Some plan. She hadn't even taken the meat out of the freezer.

'I've been trying to get hold of you all day,' he said,

unfastening Shuli from the safety restraints. 'Where on earth have you been?'

Jane belatedly discovered that she wasn't perfect wife material. She found herself wanting to ask him where he got off, talking to her like that. She wasn't his secretary any more. He wasn't paying for her time by the hour.

By reminding herself that he might, just might, have a point, she managed to restrain herself. 'Do you want the whole story, or just the edited highlights?' she asked, finally getting to her feet and pushing back the damp strands of hair that were clinging untidily to her face. She didn't wait for an answer, preferring not to confront his shocked expression at her appearance, but took the bucket through to the utility room and tipped the water down the drain.

'I think we'd better stick to the highlights for now,' he said, following her but remaining in the doorway, presumably to avoid contamination.

'Right.' She dried her hands and turned to face him. She didn't think this was the moment to tell him that Shuli had left a sticky handprint on the lapel of his dark suit. 'Well, let's see,' she began. 'This morning, after breakfast, the cleaning team arrived. What with the noise of the vacuum cleaner and being underfoot no matter where I went, it seemed like a good idea to take Shuli for a walk—explore the village, check out the post office and the village shop. You know—show myself, give people something to talk about.'

'You certainly know how to make yourself popular.'

She glanced at him uncertainly. Was that supposed to be funny? There was nothing in his expression to suggest he was clamouring to join her fan club. 'I didn't get very far before this walking hearthrug decided he wanted to come along.' He glanced at the dog but made no comment on his appearance. 'I tried to discourage him, but he would keep running out into the road so I had no choice,' Jane said, just a little desperately. 'I had to grab hold of him.'

He didn't commend her public spirit, either. 'There might have been an accident, Mark.'

'That's why you brought him home?'

'No!' Then, 'Well, yes, but that was later. When I needed the car. He didn't have a collar, you see.'

'He's got one now.'

This was like wading through treacle, Jane thought, but she refused to get upset. This was Mark's home. She'd never seen it looking less than pristine. He had every right to be angry, she reminded herself. 'I asked at the village shop and the post office and the pub but no one recognised him.'

'This tends to be a pedigree dog neighbourhood. Good-looking dalmatians and Labradors, mostly. I shouldn't think too many people around here would admit to owning this apology for a dog.'

'He's got a lovely nature,' she declared defensively. Then, realising that she was not helping things, she said, 'Yes, well, I took him to the police station. They thought he'd probably been abandoned overnight. That someone had just dumped him from a car. How could anyone do that?' she demanded.

'It beats me.' The puppy shuffled closer so that his nose was touching the toe of Mark's shoe.

'They suggested I take him to the RSPCA,' Jane said, 'but he cried so when we walked away. And then Shuli cried.'

Mark looked up. 'And then you cried?' he suggested.

'Of course not.' She blinked rapidly. She did not get sentimental over abandoned animals.

'Of course not,' he repeated, clearly unconvinced. 'So, what this short version comes right down to is that we now have a dog?'

'I don't know what else I could have done, Mark.' He shook his head as if he couldn't believe his ears. 'Are you very angry?'

'Angry?' Mark regarded the sweet, caring woman who was looking at him as if he might throw her and the dog out of the house. And felt like a heel. 'How can I be angry? You did what you always do. You saw a need and dealt with it. First Shuli, then me, then the dog.' Which sort of put him in his place.

'He's a nice dog, Daddy,' Shuli said helpfully, reaching down, wanting to touch. The dog sat up hopefully.

'It's only temporary. Until his owners turn up,' Jane offered optimistically. 'I left a phone number with the police and the RSPCA.'

'I won't hold my breath.'

'No,' she admitted. 'That probably wouldn't be wise. Is it a terrible imposition, Mark? I will find a new home for him.' She didn't actually say, If you insist, but he saw the words in her eyes.

Mark felt the tension of his own bad day melting beneath the twin assaults of two pairs of brown pleading eyes. Putting off the inevitable moment, clinging to the pretence that this would be his decision, he bent to ruffle the fur behind the pup's ears.

'He's a really nice dog, Daddy,' Shuli said, her little face furrowed with anxiety.

'I'm sure he's a very nice dog.' The dog, his immediate slave, licked his fingers. 'Have you given him a name yet?'

'Name?' Jane repeated, as if such a thing had never entered her head.

'His name is Bob,' Shuli said. 'Bob the dog. Here, Bob!' The pup wiggled ecstatically at so much attention.

Mark looked up. 'Bob?'

'It doesn't mean anything.' Jane, pink and flustered at being caught out in this act of gross sentimentality, rushed to defend herself. Things had been going so well; she didn't want to ruin it now. 'We—Shuli and I—thought he looked like a Bob. That's all.'

'Yes,' he agreed, straightening. 'He does.'

Oh, heck, he was not amused. Well, why would he be? One day—he'd been married to her for just one day—and instead of peace and tranquillity he'd got Bob. And no dinner.

'He'll need a collar and lead. And some shots,' he said. She made a sort of noise in the back of her throat. 'He's already had them?'

'The RSPCA gave him his shots and a health check before I brought him home.' For a small fee.

'Along with the collar?'

'And lead. He's been well looked after. No fleas—'

'Just surplus to requirements?'

'And a bit muddy after a night on the common.'

'And he chased a duck, Daddy. Right into the pond. There was mud—' she flung her little hands wide in a vivid demonstration '—everywhere.'

'Thank you, Shuli,' Jane said, wondering if it could get any worse. 'I can't imagine how I forgot that part.' Then she realised that, contrary to expectations, Mark was struggling not to laugh. 'I bathed him outside, but he escaped before I'd quite finished.'

'He ran inside and shook himself all over the kitchen,' Shuli added, quite unnecessarily. 'See, Daddy?' And she very kindly pointed to a splatter of mud that Jane had missed. Because it was halfway up one of the pristine white walls.

'You're sure *you* bathed *him*?'

Mark reached out and wiped his fingertips over her cheek. His hand was cool, his touch sweet bliss against her hot and bothered skin. It was all she could do not to rub herself against him and purr, say, Thank you for understanding. He held it up his fingers for her to see. 'It looks more as if he transferred the mud to you.'

She looked down at herself and groaned. So much for the well-groomed wife, the angelic infant and the exquisitely prepared dinner waiting for her hero at the end of a hard day slaying dragons.

'Don't worry, it'll wash off.' He looked around. 'Probably.' Then, 'It certainly explains why you haven't had time to check the answering machine for messages.'

'Oh, Lord! You said you'd been trying to ring me. Is something wrong?'

'You were going to ring your mother?' She clapped a hand over her mouth. 'I can see you had more important things on your mind.'

'I'll do it now. As soon as I've had a shower—'

'Too late, Jane. She called me first thing this morning. Apparently she rang you for a chat last night. One of your sisters is expecting a baby. Elizabeth?'

'Is she? That's wonderful, they've been trying for ages...' She stopped. 'Sorry. What else?'

'Oh, pretty much everything. The woman from Accounts who's leased your flat told your mother how surprised everyone was, how no one had suspected a thing. How romantic she thought it was that you'd married your boss.'

'Oh, Mark! I'm so sorry.' Then, 'What did you say?'

'What *could* I say? I told her the truth.' Jane felt the blood drain from her face. 'I told her I asked you to move in with me, but you wouldn't. So we got married.'

'Oh.' Then, 'You didn't say anything else?'

'Anything else, Jane, is our business.'

'Yes, yes, of course.' She swallowed hard. 'And she, um, accepted that?'

'That's probably overstating the case, but I explained about Shuli and that appeared to pacify her.'

He wasn't telling her everything. 'And?'

'And I suggested she and your father come to dinner so that we can get acquainted.'

# CHAPTER SEVEN

'DINNER?' Jane swallowed nervously. *'Some time,'* she said. 'You asked them to come to dinner *some time* so that you could get acquainted.' He didn't answer. 'Please tell me that you didn't ask my parents to dinner tonight.'

'Well, I will if you insist. But they'll still be here at six-thirty.' He put Shuli down so that she could stroke the dog. 'I wouldn't have asked them, Jane, but it was clear that your mother thought I had something to hide.'

'No! Why on earth would she think that?' But it explained why Mark had come home early. He hadn't been able to raise her on the phone so he'd been forced to come home to ensure there'd be something to eat. No wonder he'd been mad. She wasn't exactly over the moon herself. 'What could we possibly have to hide?' she asked, the edge to her voice sharp enough to cut glass. Then, with a little wail of anguish, 'Did you say *six-thirty*?'

'I did.'

'But that's…' She couldn't voice what she thought. Not with Shuli listening. 'That's so early!'

'The plan was to let Shuli win them round.' He looked down at the child, who was sitting on the floor chattering away to Bob. 'If they fall for her—'

'Oh, they will.' Who wouldn't love the child on sight? 'I'm sorry. I didn't mean to complain. It's really sweet of you to make such an effort, especially when I've dropped you in it so comprehensively.'

'But?' he prompted. 'I'm sure I sensed a ''but'' in there somewhere.'

She gave a little shrug. 'Well, just for future reference

you might like to make a note that I need a minimum of two weeks' notice to cook for my mother.'

'Two weeks?'

'One week to plan and one week to panic.'

'For heaven's sake, what kind of man do you take me for? I had Patsy call a caterer and order dinner for four at eight.'

'A caterer?' Jane covered her face with her hands and moaned pitifully. How could so much go wrong in one day?

'Of course. Caroline always used a caterer—'

Caroline? This marriage might not be the romance of the century but she was a person in her own right, not some pale stand-in for his dead wife. 'I am not Caroline,' she said, through gritted teeth.

'No,' he said. And with a sweeping glance that took in mud, dog and the cut-off jeans she'd worn to bath him, he made it clear that she would never measure up.

She wasn't about to try. She was her own woman.

'Caroline would never have wasted half an hour, let alone half a day, on a mongrel pup.'

'No? Well, I did tell you to advertise for the perfect woman, but you couldn't face the hassle so you settled for me. Live with it.' She tugged on her bottom lip with her teeth to stop the hot tears that threatened to overwhelm her. 'Just as I'll have to live with my mother telling me, at length, how my four beautiful sisters can cope with their children, their sparkling careers and a positive menagerie of pets and still manage to cook dinner for their parents.'

'Your sisters haven't been married for little more than twenty-four hours,' Mark returned sharply. 'Even your mother must suspect that you'd have more interesting things to do than cook.'

'Why? You went to work this morning. Business as usual.'

Mark felt as if he'd been sandbagged. What had he said

to provoke that reaction? They'd discussed what they'd do and they'd done it. Hadn't they? It occurred to him that perhaps 'discussed' was rather overstating the case. He'd said how it would be and she hadn't demurred. That didn't mean she was totally happy with the situation.

And, remembering how her face had lit up when he'd told her about her sister's baby, he wondered just how many assumptions he'd been guilty of making.

Maybe he should have spent a little more time working on the details of this arrangement and less time congratulating himself on his good fortune.

'Oka-a-ay…' he said. 'Why don't we try that again? Start from the beginning? I'll go out, drive around the village and then, when I come back, I'll say, Hi, honey, I'm home. Had a nice day? And you'll say, Don't ask, and then you'll tell me anyway, and I'll say, You think you've had a bad day? Just wait until you hear what happened to me…' He reached out and cradled her cheek, turning her face towards him. 'You wouldn't be laughing by any chance?' he asked hopefully.

'No…I mean yes…' Her cheeks flushed a hot pink. 'Actually, I don't know what I mean.' Then, 'Mark?' He waited. 'I'm really sorry about the dog.' She gestured at the kitchen. 'The mess in here.' She took a shaky breath. 'He dug a hole in your lovely garden, too.' She pulled her lips against her teeth, clearly afraid that this would be the final straw.

His garden. His kitchen. His house. And he hadn't exactly helped by walking in and demanding why she hadn't been there to answer the phone. She was his wife, not his secretary. It was time he started treating her like one.

'*Our* lovely garden, Jane. This is our home. And our dog.'

'You mean it?' Her eyes lit up. 'He can stay?'

'Whatever you want is fine by me. Honestly.' He bent

and ruffled the pup's ears. 'He is a very nice dog. Different. A slightly eccentric choice, perhaps—'

'He chose us.'

'So he did.'

'It's rather like that old nursery rhyme. The farmer needs a wife…the wife needs a dog…' She stopped, realising just in time that the rhyme didn't go quite like that. 'First you get an ugly duckling wife, and then you get a dog to match.'

He looked up, irritated by the way she'd put herself down. 'I didn't say that, nor should you. So what if neither of you ever fledge into swans? You'll make very fine ducks.'

'Well, thanks. I think.'

'Swans hiss and bite, Jane. Ducks are friendly and eager to please. I know which I'd rather live with.'

She took a deep breath, as if she might argue, then she said, 'Okay, you win the bunch of onions for the weirdest compliment of the month. But be very sure about the dog. Say the word and I'll take him back to the RSPCA right now. They'll find him a home, I'm sure. Eventually. But if he stays, he stays for good.'

Like the wife? 'He's got a home.' Mark looked around at the disordered kitchen. 'I've got a home.'

'But—'

'But nothing.' Her forehead had puckered in an anxious little frown and instinctively he reached out to smooth it away with the pad of his thumb. He didn't want her anxious, or worried. He certainly didn't want her in a stew because the kitchen, for once in its immaculate life, didn't look like a feature from some glossy magazine. On an impulse he placed a light kiss in the wide space between her eyes. 'A tidy house is a place where nothing happens, Jane,' he said, close enough to see the faint gold freckles that dusted her nose. 'Believe me. I know.'

*     *     *

The dining room was ready for their guests. Bob was behaving like a graduate from obedience school. Shuli had been fed, bathed and dressed in her pretty new frock.

Clipping back her hair in the ebony clasp, Jane critically regarded her appearance in a long mirror, smoothing the simple, unadorned grey dress over her hips before slipping the diamond ring Mark had bought her in place next to her wedding ring.

It wouldn't be enough. Her mother, already suspicious, was as sharp as knives. And her father, having spent thirty-five years in medical practice, had developed an intuitive gift for spotting when something was not quite as it should be. Which was why she'd spent the last fifteen minutes carefully eradicating any trace of her presence from the guest suite.

But she'd need to do a lot more than that to create the right impression when her mother asked to see around the house. As she undoubtedly would.

She could hear Mark outside, playing with Shuli and the puppy. She slipped into his bedroom, heart beating overtime and feeling like a guilty trespasser. But she had no time to waste worrying about that.

She put the silver-backed hairbrush she'd inherited from her grandmother on the heavy antique dressing table, adding a few hairpins and a jar of moisturiser for effect. The electric toothbrush her mother had bought her, but she'd never used, was propped conspicuously beside Mark's own toothbrush in his bathroom. Her new white towelling bathrobe was hung on the door beside its twin. His and hers.

Then she turned to the bed. The tender little kiss he'd given her had fired her imagination, and for a moment she held the slinky silk nightdress against her cheek, imagining herself wearing it. Imagining how it would feel to have Mark slip the shoestring straps from her shoulders so that it fell to the carpet, to puddle around her feet. She imagined him touching her, lifting her onto the huge bed that dominated the room—

Jolted from her dreams by the crunch of her father's car tyres against the gravel, she quickly tucked the nightdress beneath one of the pillows, leaving just a tiny trail of black silk visible to catch the alert eye. Even then she lingered, her hand against the cool fresh linen, before the sound of the doorbell sent her racing downstairs.

Mark looked up as Jane hurried down the stairs. She'd been a bundle of nerves and he was convinced that she was going to look so pale and guilty that her parents would think he was some kind of fiend. Instead her cheeks were faintly flushed, her eyes dark and sparkling—the perfect picture of a new bride.

For a moment he experienced again the same moment of shocked surprise that had seized his breath when he'd seen her first thing that morning. Before she'd realised he was there. Of looking at someone he'd worked with five days a week for the last two and a half years, a person he'd thought he knew, and realising that there was an undiscovered woman beneath the façade of the efficient secretary he'd taken for granted.

He wanted to tell her that, to let her know. He wanted to say how lovely she looked. But if he said that she'd think he was simply being kind. Nothing could be further from the truth.

'You look…special,' he said. Then, 'I thought you might have worn the same outfit as yesterday.'

'Yesterday's outfit wouldn't do, Mark. It offers too much scope for speculation. Now, this dull little dress serves a dual purpose.' She ran a hand over the flat surface of her abdomen, drawing attention to her body. The gesture was innocent of provocation and yet it concentrated his mind totally on her slender waist, the gentle flare of her hips. 'It hides nothing, comprehensively proving that you were speaking the plain, unvarnished truth when you told my mother that I'm not pregnant.'

'What? Oh, right.' He forced himself to concentrate. 'You said a dual purpose?'

'There is nothing to distract from this.' She held up her left hand and moved it so that the diamonds flashed in a beam of sunlight. 'As far as the outside world is concerned there's nothing more convincing of a man's sincerity than his generosity with pure carbon.' The doorbell sounded again but he didn't move. 'I don't think they're going away, Mark,' she prompted. Still he didn't move. 'You're really going to have to open the door.'

'I can't fool you, can I?' He stretched out his hand. 'You know I'm scared to death. Will you hold my hand?'

'Like this?' She placed her fingers on his.

'No, I think we should make it really convincing.' And he tightened his grip and pulled her close, then put his arm around her before throwing open the door.

Pressed against Mark's freshly ironed shirt, bombarded with the shock of his body hard against hers, an elusive hint of aftershave, the warmth of his hand keeping her close, Jane had to struggle for breath. 'Mum, Dad…this is Mark…'

# CHAPTER EIGHT

THERE was a moment of brittle tension while Mark shook hands with her parents. Then her mother said, 'Oh, come here.' And, gathering her up, gave her a big hug before holding her at arm's length. 'You look wonderful. And who's this?'

Shuli, hiding behind her father's legs, had to be coaxed to say hello. But then Bob hurtled through from the back of the house, wiggling with such excitement that Jane rushed him out into the garden, calling back, 'He's going to have an accident if I don't...' and grabbing the excuse to catch her breath.

Her father followed her. 'Your mother was worried, Jane,' he said, as they watched Bob chase a starling. 'I can see there was no need. I've never seen you look so happy.'

She was. It was totally pathetic that that one little kiss, Mark's arm around her waist, should make the world seem brand-new. But they had. 'Everything's—' she lifted her hands in a gesture designed to indicate that the world was a wonderful place '—perfect.'

'Then I'm delighted. I was looking forward to walking my little girl up the aisle, though.'

Fortunately Bob chose that moment to race back and show them how happy he was. 'No! Down, Bob!' She pulled him off. 'Sorry, but he's new. A stray.'

'He's going to be a handful.'

'Just a bit excited to have a new family,' Mark said, bringing out a tray with glasses and a bottle of champagne. 'I know how he feels.' He opened the bottle, poured out the wine. 'Jennifer.' Jane blinked to hear her mother addressed by her first name on such short acquaintance. 'Harry.'

'Thanks. I was just telling Jane that I'm sorry to have missed out on walking her up the aisle the way I did her sisters.'

Mark handed her a glass with a look that fried her insides. 'I just couldn't wait,' he said, and grinned broadly.

Seriously convincing if you didn't know that it was all play-acting. Like the arm about her waist, she realised.

And the evening suddenly lost its sparkle. She responded on automatic to her father's toast, just sipping the champagne before putting the glass down to pick up Shuli, make a fuss of her.

'Jane?' She looked up to discover everyone was looking at her.

'Sorry, did you say something?'

'I suggested that your parents should stay over. Back me up, here. Tell them we've got plenty of room. That it's crazy to drive all the way home tonight.'

Jane nearly choked on her champagne. Did he realise what he was doing? There was convincing, she thought, and then there was asking for trouble.

'Really, we can't,' her father said quickly, before her mother allowed herself to be persuaded. 'I have a clinic tomorrow morning. But you must come down for a weekend very soon so that you can meet the rest of the family and we can have a proper celebration. Shuli will love it. There are lots of children and we're right by the sea.'

'We can't leave Bob,' Jane said, before Mark could do something stupid like say yes.

'Bring him with you. I don't suppose one more dog will be noticed, do you? We'll soon wear him out on the beach. What about the weekend after next?'

'That sounds wonderful,' Mark said, before she could leap in with some unbeatable excuse. She was fast running out of excuses. In fact her brain had stopped functioning right after she'd worked out what the arm about the waist had really meant. 'Shuli has no cousins of her own. It'll be a whole new world for her. Just what she needs, wouldn't you say, Jane?'

It was exactly what she'd been saying. Shuli needed a family and her family was the one she'd had in mind. It would have been perfect, but for one small detail.

Fortunately her father made any reply unnecessary. 'You have no immediate family, Mark?' he asked.

'A mother and sister, both too busy putting the world to rights to have much time to spare for mundane things like family life. Shuli's mother was an only child. Her parents were killed when she was a baby; her grandmother raised her. So it's just been the two of us.' He glanced at Jane. 'Until now.'

'Well, maybe Shuli will have a new brother or sister of her own very soon,' her mother suggested.

'For heaven's sake, Jennifer, let the girl catch her breath.' And her lovely, lovely father, well-practised in the art of changing the subject, said, 'This is a lovely old house, Mark. Not what I'd expected at all. I've seen some of your designs and I imagined you'd be living in some minimalist ultra-modern affair constructed from glass and steel. A functional advertisement for your work.'

Only Jane was situated to see the briefest look of pain flicker across Mark's features before he said, 'If you'll excuse me, I'll go and see what's happening about dinner.'

'And I'll put Shuli to bed. Mum, do you want to come and give me a hand? See the house?'

Jane leaned back against the door. 'Well, that was different.'

'I enjoyed myself,' Mark said. 'They're nice people.'

'I never suggested they weren't. Just that my mother has high expectations that I've never quite lived up to. But what would you have done if they'd accepted your invitation to stay overnight? Since the guest suite is occupied?'

She didn't wait for his answer. He'd undoubtedly got it all worked out and she didn't want to hear how she could so easily have hidden out in one of the small rooms on the top floor for tonight and no one would have known a thing about it. Instead, she kicked off her shoes and padded barefoot into the living room to set about gathering the coffee cups.

'Leave that. Come and put your feet up for a minute.' He settled on the sofa, patting the seat beside him. But Jane wasn't in the mood to get cosy. They were on their own; there was no one around he had to convince with his happy families act.

The small touches, the quick conspiratorial smiles. He'd been so good at it. Her parents hadn't suspected a thing. Now it was just the two of them. Platonically linked, until death did them part. No more need to pretend.

Until the weekend after next.

'More to the point,' she continued scratchily, her throat aching from a totally stupid desire to cry. She'd brought this entirely upon herself, after all. 'What are you going to do on our long meet-the-family weekend? You do realise that we'll be installed in state in the guest bedroom?'

He took his time, apparently giving the matter considerable thought. 'Wear pyjamas?' he offered finally.

That was it. She'd had enough. 'You're right, this can wait until the morning. I'm going to bed. Don't forget to let Bob out for a run.'

She was halfway to the door before it occurred to her that she sounded exactly like a wife. One whose husband needn't think that she'd be awake when he followed her up the stairs.

Very apt.

'Jane—' She turned in the doorway. Mark had put his

feet up on the sofa and with his hands laced behind his head was stretched out with his eyes closed. 'Sleep well.'

Mark couldn't sleep. He'd forgotten how it felt to have a woman burning mad at him. The boiling mixture of emotions that could be blown away in the kind of sex that started as a fight and ended in hot, sweet, forgive-me lovemaking.

And the only woman he had in his head was Jane.

He didn't understand it. A week ago he'd scarcely been aware of Jane as a woman at all. Now her scent clung to him, even here in his own bed, evoking the silk of her skin against his fingers.

That flash of anger in her eyes when he'd mentioned Caroline. The soft, dark look of surprise when he'd kissed the frown from her forehead. And his mind just wouldn't let go of that early-morning picture, of full soft lips just begging to be kissed.

How many times today had he come close to kissing her? Just taking her in his arms and kissing her with no thought of the past? Half a dozen times. And when she'd stormed up to bed it had taken every ounce of will-power not to follow her and suggest they give the double bed a practise run.

He gave up on sleep and flung himself out of bed to pace the carpet.

That kind of response didn't happen overnight. Not with someone you'd known for years. It had to have been there, growing unseen, like bulbs forced into flower for Christmas. Kept in the dark while they built up a strong root system, they burst into flower within days of being brought into the light.

Jane wasn't conventionally beautiful. She wasn't the kind of girl who'd ever turn heads. But her kindness and generosity were qualities that touched even the most moribund of hearts and, unlike beauty, would never fade. They already had the LTR, a long-term relationship based on trust and respect. It had simply needed light to flower into something deeper.

Now all he had to do was find some way to demonstrate his feelings. And to help Jane forget whatever pain had driven her to contemplate a platonic marriage.

He remembered what she'd said about diamonds. Guaranteed to convince. But that was to convince other people. No, it needed a larger, more personal gesture, something that she couldn't possibly misinterpret.

As he turned he stepped on something sharp. A hairpin. He bent and picked it up. Then looked around. Jane had been in here? That was why her scent lingered in the air?

He groaned as he realised that she must have scattered her possessions around to convince her mother. Her brush, her hairpins. He crossed swiftly to the bed and, pulling off the pillows, was assailed by the delicate scent she'd been wearing. Her nightdress. Her nightdress had been here in his bed. The very thought of it inflamed a passion he'd thought long dead.

Reaching for his robe, he went down to his study. He might as well catch up with work. There was no way he was sleeping tonight.

# CHAPTER NINE

'MARRIED life is a lot tougher than it looks,' Jane said in response to Laine's question. She tucked the telephone into her shoulder, taking advantage of Shuli's absence at play-group to tidy Mark's office as she talked. He must have been looking for something to show her father because there were blueprints heaped up everywhere. 'My parents came to dinner last night.'

'I know. Your mother rang my mother and I'm seriously in the doghouse for not spilling the beans. I hope it's worth it.' Then, when Jane didn't respond with instant glee, 'From the resounding silence I take it you're still in the spare room?'

'Please! The guest suite. But you're right; it isn't going to happen overnight. In fact my plan of proving myself the perfect wife didn't survive the first day.'

'You've had a row?'

'Yes. No. Maybe.'

'That was decisive.'

'It wasn't about anything personal.' Well, it had felt pretty personal when she'd been compared to Caroline and found wanting, but that was her business. 'It all began when I found this stray dog.'

'Crumbs, Jane. Whatever possessed you?' Laine demanded, when she'd finished telling her the entire story. 'Can't you ever just look the other way?'

Like Caroline? 'Apparently not.'

'Well, I think your Mark is a hero and you can tell him so from me. Give him a great big kiss as well.'

'You haven't heard the worst, yet. We've been invited home for the weekend. A full-dress family affair.'

'Is that a problem?'

'Think about it, Laine.'

'Oh, you mean you're going to have to share that great big double bed. Some problem. Why are you waiting until next weekend? Drag him down there tomorrow. And don't forget to pack your sexy black nightdress.'

'I don't just want sex, Laine. I want him to love me.'

'Darling, you wear the nightdress, you let your hair hang loose and you just stand there. He won't be able to help himself. Trust me.' Then, 'How's that sweet little girl?'

'Totally gorgeous. She's at playgroup right now.' Then, 'She woke me up this morning to ask if she could call me Mummy.'

'Oh, Jane!' Then, 'Did you cry?'

She sniffed. 'I'm crying right now.'

'So am I.'

Promising to ring again soon, Jane replaced the receiver on the handset and bent down to pick up a piece of blueprint that had been ripped up and tossed in the bin.

It wasn't for anything very big. It didn't have a project number or name, only 'Detached House, Upper Haughton' printed in the corner. And the date. It was five, no, six years old.

Jane retrieved the rest of it, but she knew where it was even before she'd pieced together the drawing of the front elevation. She'd passed it that morning as she'd taken Shuli to the village hall.

She might not have noticed the house at all, hidden behind an old weathered brick wall, but as she'd passed the gate the woman who lived there had come out with her own two little ones and had stopped to say hello. And then Jane had seen the house and admired it.

'We were so lucky. It was exactly what we were looking for, although I suppose it's not to everyone's taste. It was built specially as a surprise for the architect's bride-to-be, but she'd set her heart on a Georgian rectory she'd seen. And that apparently was that.'

She'd known even then that it must have been designed by Mark. Now, looking at the drawing he'd poured his heart into, Jane wanted to weep all over again.

'The playgroup is holding a jumble sale on Saturday, Mark. I've sorted through my things, but I wondered if you'd got anything past its wear-by date in your wardrobe. It's for a good cause. We're raising money for some outdoor play equipment.'

Mark glanced up. For days there had been a brittle, touch-me-not distance about Jane. Everything she did was pitch-perfect, there had been no more incidents with stray dogs, or mud on the kitchen walls, but something was wrong. He just couldn't pin her down long enough to find out what it was. Every time he tried to talk to her she leapt up to do something that apparently couldn't wait a second.

He'd hoped that prompting Shuli to call her Mummy would have opened the emotional barriers. She'd been affected by it, he knew; he'd seen the tears. But it hadn't been enough. Even now she could hardly wait for his answer so that she could race off and be doing something, anything, rather than putting her feet up and spending the evening with him.

'Don't say I didn't warn you. Once you're on the jumble sale rota your life will never be your own. Have they got you on the village hall committee yet?'

'I'm not helping, Mark. Not this time,' she said, avoiding a direct answer. 'We're going away for the weekend. Remember?'

'Of course. Better hang on to any pyjamas you find, then,' he added. He knew he shouldn't, but he just couldn't stop himself.

'You've actually got some?' she enquired, ultra-polite.

'I couldn't swear to it.'

Jane was struggling to hold herself together. Until she'd seen that plan she hadn't had any idea of what she was up against. How much he'd loved Caroline. How utterly futile it was to imagine he would ever love her. And nothing less would do. 'We don't have to go, Mark,' she said, hoping that he would grab the lifeline. 'I could make up some excuse.'

'No, they're expecting us. It's supposed to be a secret but they're planning a huge party.' He'd been talking to her parents? He must have seen her confusion because he added, 'Harry phoned and asked if I wanted to go fishing.'

'Oh.'

'Don't look so tragic,' he said. 'I promise I won't snore—'

She snatched the paper out of his hands. 'Stop it! Will you stop being flip and take this seriously?'

'It's *serious*? I thought it was just a jumble sale. Okay, well, you'll find a load of Caroline's clothes in one of the spare rooms. Take those. I'm sure they'll cause a lot more excitement than my old shirts.'

She looked stunned. She might well do. He was fairly stunned himself. That had come out of nowhere. It was right—he should have done it a long time ago—but the fact that he could do it so easily now was faintly shocking.

'Is that serious enough for you?'

For a moment she just stood there, and then she turned and walked away. He heard her mount the stairs, then go up again to the top floor, where there were half a dozen small rooms that were mostly used for storage. He heard her opening doors until she found the one with the rails of designer clothes that had belonged to Caroline.

He poured two large drinks and then went after her.

'Jane?' She'd pulled the dust covers from the rails and was looking at the clothes. He offered her a glass. She took it without saying a word, didn't even appear to notice that their fingers had touched. Didn't so much as twitch, let alone jump like the nervous kitten she'd been all week. He was the one who felt as if his skin had been seared. She swallowed a mouthful of brandy and shuddered. 'This lot should cause a bit of a stir in jumble sale circles,' he offered.

Jane had expected a few bags of clothes. Designer labels, of course. There'd been nothing 'chainstore' about Caroline Hilliard. Tall, slender, with a personal fortune that had allowed her to indulge her taste in fine things, she'd caused a stir wherever she went, apparently. But it was a shock to confront the reality. She couldn't conceive of any woman owning so many beautiful clothes.

'You can't...I can't...' She gave up. She didn't know what to say.

'Can't what? They're just clothes. Would you wear any of them?' Jane shook her head. Took a step back. 'Of course you wouldn't.'

Afraid she'd offended him in some way, Jane said, 'They wouldn't fit me, Mark.' Not in any sense, she thought.

'No,' he said. And she shrank inwardly. She was way out of her depth here. And in grave danger of making a fool of herself. He must never know how she felt about him. That scrap of dignity was all she had left. 'She was a lot taller than you.' A lot more everything, Jane thought as he bent to pick up a shoe. 'And she had feet to match.' Long, narrow, elegant feet.

'Talk about her, Mark. Tell me about her.' *Lay the ghost.*

'You want to know about Caroline?' She didn't want to know about her. She didn't want to ever hear her name on his lips. But until his first wife was out in the open, all the dark shadows exposed to the light, their marriage would remain a sham. 'Caroline is what you see about you, Jane,' he said at last. 'The house, the clothes. Perfection in everything. It was, in the end, her need for perfection that killed her.'

Jane frowned. 'But she drowned...'

'She was suffering from post-natal depression, Jane. It wasn't an accident.'

'Oh…' She shivered. 'I had no idea. Poor woman. Poor Shuli.' And then, 'Poor you.'

He replaced the shoe and then put an arm around her shoulder and said, 'Come on, let's go back downstairs.' He paused in the doorway, looked back, then turned out the light. 'I'll get this lot cleared out tomorrow.'

'No.' She looked up at him. 'Leave it to me. I'll do it. But not to the jumble sale. I don't want Caroline talked about, her things picked over.' Having Mark meet someone in the village wearing her clothes. 'It wouldn't be…proper.'

'I'm not sure either of us deserve such thoughtfulness from you, Jane. But thank you.'

Back in the softly lit drawing room, Mark topped up their glasses. 'We were the golden couple, did you know that?' he asked, with just a trace of bitterness. He didn't expect an answer because he went on, 'We had everything. Money, recognition, style. And for a while it was enough. Then Caroline decided she had to have a baby, too. All her friends had babies. It was the ultimate accessory. They glowed, they gave birth and then passed the result to a nanny to care for. They made it look so easy.'

Jane shivered, stirred, looked at Mark. 'What about you?'

'Me? I was delighted, over the moon. It was like the world had been made over just for me.' He took a long drink. 'The first few months were fine. She told all her friends, basked in the attention, read all the books. She was going to be the perfect mother. Then—' he shook his head. 'I don't know. She just seemed to panic. It had been exciting for a while, but then reality kicked in and she wanted to turn it all off. She couldn't.'

'What a nightmare.'

'She blamed me, of course. And she was right. She was like a beautiful piece of perfect glass. Exquisite, but fragile.

I should have known she'd never cope. That she was just playing—'

'Mark…' she warned. She was sure he didn't mean to be saying this. But he didn't seem to hear her. Maybe it had all been bottled up so long that it was unstoppable.

'She hadn't had much morning sickness to speak off, but suddenly she started to be sick with nerves. I've never felt so helpless in my life.' He stared into the depths of his glass. 'The last three months were undiluted hell, but I thought once the baby arrived everything would be better. If anything they were worse. She just lost interest in everything. I even had to wash her hair…'

Jane fought the lump in her throat. She must not cry. He needed her to be strong. To listen and absolve him…

'She wouldn't touch Shuli. Could hardly bear to look at her. She had a maternity nurse, but she couldn't be on call twenty-four hours a day. I did what I could but the work was piling up. Maybe if she'd had a mother it would have been different.'

Jane thought of her own capable mother, how she'd been there for her sisters. Was always there. A lifeline. 'Yes,' she said. 'A mother makes all the difference.'

'She was totally unable to cope with this small helpless creature who was totally dependent upon her. She was desperate to escape. When some friends suggested she join them for a couple of weeks in the Mediterranean she begged to go with them. God help me, I thought it would do her good. The sun, swimming… She loved to swim.'

'It could have been an accident, Mark. Even the strongest swimmers get into difficulty.'

'That was the Coroner's verdict,' he conceded. 'But she'd sent me a letter. Taken it to the post office and sent it by special delivery so that she could be sure it would arrive. By the time I got it, she was dead.'

'Mark, I'm so sorry.'

He acknowledged her sympathy, but his smile never

reached his eyes. 'It was the last act of a perfectionist. Leaving a note would have been far too messy. It would have meant everyone knowing that she'd failed the ultimate test for a woman. Motherhood. The letter was not for public consumption, just to say sorry...'

'Mark, she didn't fail. She needed help—'

'Not a holiday?' He stood up. 'Yes. I'm making no excuses, the failure was mine. As a husband.' He reached out, grasped her hand. 'I promise I'll try harder this time, Jane.'

For a moment she believed he was going to reach out for her, hold on to her, seeking some kind of reassurance, forgiveness. If he did that, anything was possible. But he turned away—almost, she thought, with relief—as Shuli called out from her room. 'She's excited about tomorrow. Meeting all her new cousins. Would you mind going up to her? I'll take Bob for a walk.'

She wanted to scream with frustration, but she could see that he needed to be alone for a while with his thoughts. So she just said, 'Try and keep him out of the pond.'

# CHAPTER TEN

JANE sat at the window seat by the open window. The night was soft and warm, and beneath her the honeysuckle and night-scented stocks filled her mother's moon-silvered garden with sweetness.

Mark had stayed tactfully downstairs, using the excuse of taking Bob out for a walk before joining her. Giving her an opportunity to get into bed, close her eyes and pretend to be asleep. He couldn't believe she'd manage the real thing.

She'd scarcely had a moment to talk with him all day. She'd waited last night for him to come back, but he must have walked for a long time with his memories for company. Bob had been worn out, totally ignoring the jangling of his lead when she'd taken Shuli to playgroup that morning.

And the child had claimed all her attention in the car on their way to her parents'. Stories, games—the journey had passed in a flash. And once they'd arrived—well, there had been dinner and family news to catch up on. Elizabeth's news to wonder over. A dozen people for Mark to meet.

Finally, though, they were to be alone. She had it all planned. All he had to do was kiss her. She'd do the rest. She started slightly as she heard the lightest warning tap on the door before he opened it. Her heart was pounding like a road drill, her skin heating up...

'Are you asleep?' And then, as he saw her, 'Oh...'

'Don't turn the light on,' she murmured. She didn't turn around. 'There's a fox in the garden.' She reached back, holding out her hand to him. 'Come and see.'

For a long moment she thought he wouldn't come, but

then his hand grasped hers and he put a knee on the seat beside her to look out of the small casement window and search the shadows. 'Where?'

'Just there.' He leaned closer, his chest pressed against her back, his soft twill shirt against her skin. He smelled so good, felt so strong... 'She's got her cubs with her.' She retrieved her hand to point to the dark patch on the grass where they were playing and he put his hand on her shoulder. Palm against naked skin. Surely he could hear the sizzle? She turned to look up at him. 'Do you see, Mark?' she said.

His face was unreadable in the moonlight, just black and white shadows like the negative of an old picture that might be anybody... 'Yes,' he said. 'I see.' Then he bent and kissed her, so gently, so tenderly, so briefly that before she could respond it was over. 'Go to bed, Jane.'

'Mark...'

'Tomorrow, Jane. Go. I won't disturb you.'

Too late for that. She was disturbed beyond endurance. But she didn't need telling twice. Grateful for the darkness to hide her hot shame, she scrambled from the window seat and into bed, lying on the farthest edge, her back turned towards him. But she needn't have bothered; he kept his word, sitting at the window, staring out into the night.

As for tomorrow—what difference would a day make? He'd made his position clear right from the beginning while she, in her vanity, had believed she could win his heart.

'Mum, can I talk to you?'

'Goodness, Jane, aren't you ready? We're meeting the girls in less than an hour.'

'It's Saturday lunchtime down the pub. It hardly calls for designer dressing.' She realised belatedly that mother was, in fact, dressed to kill. 'Isn't it?'

'We haven't gone to all the trouble of getting the men and the children out of our hair just for an hour at the pub, sweetheart. Elizabeth has found an absolutely wonderful new restaurant for our own little hen party treat and it's definitely not a jeans kind of place. Why don't you wear that lovely outfit you wore for your wedding?'

'No…'

'Please, make an effort, Jane. Your sisters always do.'

'For heaven's sake, Mum! I've probably made the biggest mistake in my life and all you're interested in is whether I can hold my own in the fashion stakes with my sisters. We both know it's a waste of time even trying.'

'Mistake?'

'Mark doesn't love me. I thought I could make him…' As her mother reached for her the whole truth spilled out in a torrent of anguished self-pity. 'What on earth am I going to do?'

'Do?' Her mother touched her cheek. 'You don't need me to tell you what you have to do, darling. You're going to go upstairs right now, put on your make-up and your pretty new clothes—'

'I can't—'

'Yes, Jane. You can. You have no choice. They need you. Mark made an honest bargain with you, and you have taken on a little girl who loves you—'

'And I love her.'

'Of course you do. As I love you. And I know you won't let either of them down.'

'No.'

'This might not be a great romance, Jane, but marriage takes a lot more than romance. It takes hard work and commitment. And sometimes a brave face.'

'I hope I'm as good a mother to Shuli as you have always been to us.'

'I used to worry about you so much, but I must have done something right. You're strong, Jane. Inside—where it matters. You'll be a wonderful mother to Shuli. And you'll have babies of your own, too. Just give it time.'

'How long?'

'How long is a piece of string?' Her mother looked at her watch and gave a little yelp of panic. 'Let's take this one step at a time. Right now, you've got twenty minutes.'

'Why are we stopping?' Jane looked around as her mother pulled into a space in front of the church. 'Why are all these cars here?'

'The Women's Institute…' she said vaguely, as if that were explanation enough. 'I've just remembered that I promised to pass on a message. I won't be a minute. Why don't you go and have a little chat to your grandmother? You always used to tell her your troubles when you were little.'

'You think she'll have the answer?'

Her mother, about to climb out of the car, paused and put her hand over Jane's. 'It wouldn't hurt to ask.'

'No.' Jane got out of the car and walked around the church to the quiet spot where her grandmother was buried.

Someone else was there before her.

'Mark?' He turned as she approached. 'I thought you'd all gone down to the beach.' But he wasn't dressed for the beach. He was wearing a cream suit. A shirt the same colour as her *shalwar kameez*. A new tie she'd bought him. 'What are you doing here? What's going on?'

'Last night—'

'Don't!'

'Last night I wanted to make love with you, Jane. More than anything in the world. I ached with a depth of longing, desire, that I was certain I'd never feel for any woman ever again.'

That wasn't an answer. But she'd lost interest in her original question. 'Then why didn't you? I couldn't have made myself plainer—'

'Because I'd done everything wrong.'

'No!'

'Oh, yes. I'd seized your selfless offer with both hands without a second thought. That should have told me something, don't you think? What man would marry a girl he didn't care for? I could have hired a housekeeper or a live-in nanny any time in the last two and a half years, but I didn't want to share my house with anyone. Yet from the moment you said ''Are you asking me if I'd marry you?'' I never considered anything else. It seemed so...right.'

'I pushed you into it. I knew you'd never advertise, but I thought if I put the idea into your head—'

'I was so sure it was the right thing to do, and I told myself that you must have a good reason to settle for something less than perfect. I imagined that someone had broken your heart, too, and you couldn't ever face the pain again.' He took her hand. 'That wasn't the reason, was it?'

Jane was without defences. Only the truth would serve her now. 'There has only ever been one love in my life, Mark. I've loved you from the first moment I saw you.'

'And I think I must have loved you for a long time. Maybe from that first day when you walked into my life, picked up Shuli and cuddled her, stopped her fretting.'

He remembered? 'A helpless, needy man and his baby,' she said softly. 'I knew you'd both break my heart even then. Well, last night I finally felt the pain.'

'Last night was different.'

'How, Mark? How was it different?'

'Because I wanted to make a gesture. Show you how much you really mean to me. Make a new start. Not as some couple who married out of convenience and fell into bed because it was there...' He took both her hands and clasped them in his. 'Everyone we both know and care for is waiting in the church. To hear us say our vows before God. To bless our marriage not as an expedient but as a partnership, in every sense of the word.'

'A blessing?' She looked around at all the cars. 'You've arranged all this?'

'With the help of your parents, your sisters, and Laine. I've even managed to drag my mother and sister here for the occasion. I love you, Jane, and I want everyone to know it. You're my wife in name. Now I'm asking you will you be my wife...' he paused briefly, as if searching for the right words '...heart, body and soul?'

She reached up, touched his face. 'I always was, my love. I've just been waiting for you to notice.'

'Then let's not keep the vicar waiting.'

Laine and Shuli were waiting for them in the porch. Laine hugged her and handed her a bouquet of flowers. Shuli had a velvet cushion waiting to carry their wedding rings.

And when, after they'd exchanged their vows, the vicar said, 'You may kiss the bride,' Mark's tender, lingering kiss held a promise that this was the real beginning of their marriage.

Jane turned and picked up Shuli. Mark took her, and with his hand in hers walked her down the aisle. At the church door he stopped to kiss her again. 'You know,' he murmured, 'I really like your family, but I don't think I want to spend my honeymoon with them.'

'We could go home.'

'We could,' he agreed. 'Or we could leave Shuli and Bob with your parents while we go to Paris for a few days.' And he opened his jacket so that she alone could see the airline tickets in his inside pocket. 'What do you think, Mrs Hilliard?'

'I think I'm the luckiest woman in the world.'

He reached up, brushed a tear from her cheek. 'No. The bravest, truest, strongest woman. The luck is all mine.'

'Daddy?'

'Yes, angel?'

'*Now* can I have a baby brother?'

Mark glanced at Jane, lifting his eyebrow, and she blushed. 'We'll work on it, sweetheart. I promise you, we'll work on it.'

# There are 24 timeless classics in the Mills & Boon® 100th Birthday Collection

*Two of these beautiful stories are out each month. Make sure you collect them all!*

Plus *A Perfect Proposal* by Liz Fielding, this fantastic bonus story, exclusive to WHSmith!